PROPHETESS

Prophetess

A NOVEL

Baharan Baniahmadi

ESPLANADE BOOKS

THE FICTION IMPRINT AT VÉHICULE PRESS

ESPLANADE BOOKS IS THE FICTION IMPRINT AT VÉHICULE PRESS

Published with the generous assistance of the Canada Council for the Arts, the Canada Book Fund of the Department of Canadian Heritage, and the Société de développement des entreprises culturelles du Québec (SODEC).

Canadä̈   *SODEC*
                Québec ✦✦

 Canada Council   Conseil des arts
                    for the Arts   du Canada

This novel is a work of fiction. Any resemblance to people or events is coincidental and unintended by the author.

Esplanade Books editor: Dimitri Nasrallah
Cover design: David Drummond
Typeset in Minion and Filosofia
Printed by Livres Rapido Books

LIBRARY AND ARCHIVES CANADA CATALOGUING IN PUBLICATION

Title: Prophetess : a novel / Baharan Baniahmadi.
Names: Baniahmadi, Baharan, 1984- author.
Identifiers: Canadiana (print) 20220157693 | Canadiana (ebook) 20220157839 | ISBN 9781550655957 (softcover) | ISBN 9781550656015 (HTML)
Classification: LCC PS8603.A622 P76 2022 | DDC C813/.6—dc23

Published by Véhicule Press, Montréal, Québec, Canada

Distribution in Canada by LitDistCo
www.litdistco.ca

Distribution in US by Independent Publishers Group
www.ipgbook.com

Printed in Canada on FSC certified paper.

For my father,
who always encouraged artistry.

For my brother,
who taught me about equality.

PART ONE

Passive Aggressive

1

"A GIRL SHOULDN'T LAUGH out loud." This is what Setayesh tells me when she sees me on the floor, crying from laughter. "Get up! Your skirt has moved a little! I can see your body parts!" she says. I laugh as if the whole world is muted except my voice. Setayesh laughs and tickles me. There is no sound in the universe other than our laughter. Setayesh says, "You are too loud, sis! You are too talkative."

Maman is in the kitchen, as always. She says, "Go out and play in the alley, you spoiled kids. I am not in the mood. Didn't I tell you to go out and play whenever Baba has guests? You're too loud! Your voices are everywhere. You can be heard throughout the whole neighbourhood!"

Maman is crying. I don't know why. I want to ask Setayesh why Maman cries when we have guests, but I won't ask her. I ask another question instead.

"Setayesh, why do we have to leave the house whenever Baba has guests?"

Setayesh holds my hand. "Let's go, little sister. It is because we're still kids; I mean, you are still a kid and shouldn't be around Baba's friends. Although I'm older and a lady now, I'll come with you because you are still a kid."

"Why can't we be around Baba's friends? Why doesn't Uncle Shahram bring Soheila and Ladan so that we can play?"

"Because they're also women, and men need to be alone."

"But Maman's home."

"She has to cook the food."

"Once she is done cooking."

"She has to clean up."

I look at her. Setayesh pulls her hair back, shakes her skirt, and asks, "Can you braid my hair?"

"Nope."

She purses her lips. "No problem, I didn't know how to do braids when I was your age. Let me braid your hair so that it doesn't get in your face. It's too hot."

I want to braid Setayesh's hair, but I don't know how. Setayesh says we must put our hair up in the summer so that we don't sweat. She braids my hair and blows on my sweaty head and says, "I have to blow on it so that you won't get a heat rash, my girl."

"But I'm not your girl."

"Because I'm older, I have to take care of you."

I like the wind against the back of my neck. Setayesh's hair is around her neck and the heat has made it look curly. The hair on the back of her neck is sweaty. I don't know how to braid her hair.

Setayesh says, "I know you're little and don't know how to braid. That's fine, I won't get mad at you." She tries to braid her own hair but her hands can't reach. "I messed up," she laughs.

I laugh too.

She asks, "Do the curly ends look better?"

"Yes, sister, your hair looks beautiful. I wish my hair looked like yours." I stare at Setayesh's curly hair. It's down to her shoulders. Setayesh is the prettiest girl in our neighbourhood. In a couple of years, my hair will be as long as Setayesh's, and I will pull my bangs back when they get in my face, just like Setayesh does. I will be as tall as Setayesh. I want to be like Setayesh. Be prettier than everyone else. We are sitting on the doorstep, and Setayesh is making shapes with the shadow of her hands. I laugh.

"You are my little sister," says Setayesh as she kisses me.

I love her. She loves me so much. Her face is soft when she kisses me. It's not rough like Baba's beard, or dry like Maman's hand. Setayesh and I are making animals with the shadow of our hands and then imitating their sounds.

"How does the wolf sound? Baa…baa…"

"Don't try to fool me. The wolf?" I laugh.

Setayesh makes a serious face and says that the wolf sounds like the sheep. They both go, baa…baa…

"Nope, let's go ask Maman."

"No, we can't go to Maman. We need to stay out for the rest of the night."

"What if it's hot?"

"We still need to stay out. We can drink some water."

"What if we get hungry?"

"I don't know, maybe we could eat something."

"But we don't have money."

"I don't know…"

It is hot. In our part of Tehran, the heat is always heavy. The alley in front of our house is very narrow. Our neighbourhood is small. We all know each other. Earthy walls and earthy ground, our neighbourhood smells like soil and has the colour of khaki. "What colour is khaki exactly?" I've asked Maman, Baba, and Setayesh a number of times, but every time they respond with "khaki is khaki." And I insist, "What does khaki mean? What does it mean that our neighbourhood is khaki? Grey? Cream-coloured? What colour?" Baba once said, "Our neighbourhood is the colour of misery. Now go outside and play!" And then I went outside and watched kids play hopscotch on earthy grounds.

So misery is khaki.

What colour is misery? Maman says I ask too many questions and I need to leave her alone. Setayesh and I sit on the ground outside, and she keeps making faces for me. Our clothes get dirty. I know we will get beaten tonight.

"Make wolf sounds."

"Baa...baa..." The sound doesn't come from Setayesh.

"Who is it?" Setayesh and I ask together. We look back. Uncle Moji is behind us making sheep noises.

Setayesh says, "Didn't I tell you that? Sheep do sound like wolves. Right, Uncle?"

"You are such good girls, sitting outside and playing, pretty as two pieces of candy."

"Hello, Uncle," I say.

Uncle Moji knocks on the door. Baba comes to the door, hugs Uncle Moji and invites him in. Setayesh looks at them.

"Won't these two get hot in the sun?" asks Uncle Moji.

Unlike Uncle Moji, Baba hasn't noticed us there, nor does he hear Uncle Moji's words. He says, "Come in, my wife has prepared juice for you."

Uncle Moji goes inside. "Ya Allah," he says as he goes in. "I've come here with your medicine."

"I swear to God, you are just like a brother to us! Thank you for your kindness," Baba says.

"If you need anything, let me know."

Setayesh looks at them and says to me, "Don't look inside the house."

"What does 'Ya Allah' mean?"

"When men enter somewhere indoors, they say 'Ya Allah' to announce their entrance, so that if there is a woman without a hijab, she has the time to put on a scarf."

"So 'Ya Allah' means I have arrived?"

"No, 'Ya Allah' in Arabic means God Almighty! Our theology teacher has taught us this."

"So why do we need to speak in Arabic?"

"Because if you believe in God and you are a good Muslim, you must speak Arabic better than Persian."

It doesn't make sense, but I understand. Religious people use Arabic often, phrases like 'Allah Akbar' and 'Alhamdulillah'.

Setayesh looks at me and says, "If we use Persian words, we are not good Muslims." She says, "Let's go to the main street."

We go to the main street. We walk in the shadows to avoid feeling the heat. Ali the supermarket owner and his kids are sitting by the store eating ice cream. Setayesh takes me to the front of the store because that way Ali will give us ice cream out of pity. Ali comes to the door and asks us to come inside because the air conditioner is on and outside is too hot. We go in and sit next to Ali's kids. Ali's store is small. I don't know why it seemed bigger to me just a few years ago, when I measured the store with my feet. It was much bigger, even more that twenty feet, but now it's only eighteen feet. Setayesh says it is actually sixteen feet. She measures with her own feet, but this time the store is fifteen feet. The next time she measures, it is fourteen feet. I laugh but she is annoyed. Why does Ali's store keep changing?

"We'll count the tiles then," she says.

One… two… three… Ali calls his sons. Setayesh and I watch his sons eating ice cream. All the goods in the store are on shelves. I'm afraid they'll fall on our heads. I've always been afraid of that, but it's never happened because everyone moves cautiously in the store. Ali does not bring up at all that we want ice cream.

I reach for the refrigerator and whisper to Setayesh: "Yellow soda?"

"Moron! It's Canada Dry, not yellow soda," she replies.

I grab a bottle of Canada Dry. Setayesh tries to open the bottle with her teeth, but it doesn't open. It's cold. Setayesh asks me to get a spoon from the back.

Ali's two sons look at us. One of them says, "I like your voice!"

I'm surprised. He's the first person to say so.

Ali stays beside the fridge and we are not able to get spoons.

"There's no sign of ice cream. Let's go," Setayesh says.

We run to the house laughing as I hide a soda

bottle under my dress. Setayesh takes my hand. It is sweaty. Her hands are always wet, but I like it. They're soft, not rough like Maman's hands. Whenever the three of us go out, I always want to take Setayesh's hand, but Maman pokes me and says *take my hand or you'll get lost*, and I still take Setayesh's hand while she takes Maman's as we cross the street.

Setayesh wants to leave me at the house all alone. She says that I can't come play with Samaneh and her friends because I'm too little. If she goes and plays with Samaneh, I'll stay alone and she'll forget about me. I start crying. I have this way of convincing people. I can cry whenever I need to. It's time to cry. I have to cry seriously, in a way no one will suspect. My whole face gets hot. I can't breathe. Setayesh kisses me, sees that I'm breathless and blows on my face as she says, "I won't leave you alone. Just stop crying."

I eventually take a very loud breath. She hugs me, but her long hair gets in my mouth, and I push her. But her hands are soft. She holds my face in her hands and I rub my cheeks against them. Setayesh has the softest skin in the whole world, and I like it. It's time to stop crying.

"I'm sorry," she says. "Let's go play wherever you want, just the two of us."

"Football."

"But football is for boys. Girls are not allowed to play."

I cry louder and scream this time.

"Okay, don't cry. We're going to play football." She kisses my wet face.

"Look! Look! There's a centipede on the ground." There's a centipede on the roadside near our house, where the dirt road and the asphalt road are divided to indicate the difference between the rich and the poor. The centipede lives in peace. "Do centipedes really have a thousand feet?" I ask.

"I don't know, but Baba once told me they don't."

"Then how many feet do they have?"

"No one knows. The scientists don't have time to count their feet. I just know that they have too many."

"Let's count."

"We can't. We're too far away from it. We need to get closer."

"Let's get closer." We get in close enough to count the centipede's feet. One two three four five… "Tell the centipede to stop moving, I can't count its feet when it's moving."

"Let me hold it still." Setayesh holds the centipede, but it keeps moving. "Hurry up, it is tickling me!" One two three… Setayesh throws the centipede. "We can't count its feet from up close. It tickles us. It doesn't want us to know how many feet it has. This is the secret of centipedes; they won't let us count their feet."

"Why?"

"I don't know, sis! But they have secrets just like people do."

"Will people's secrets always remain secret?"

"No, sis. All secrets are revealed one day."

"What does it mean to be revealed?"

"It means that everybody will find out."

"How do you know that?"

"Our theology teacher said that. One day, when it's the day of resurrection, all the secrets will be known and all the rewards and punishments will be given."

"So Ali the owner of the supermarket will find out that we stole the Canada Dry?"

"Mmm… not sure. Children's secrets will stay between God and us!"

"Because children are innocent?"

"Yes."

I know I am a kid. But I know I am not innocent. I can fake anything. I can fake crying, fake happiness, fake sadness. I want to ask Setayesh if I am innocent, but I ask another question instead. "Will they find out the secret of the centipede?"

"I don't know, but I guess so."

"Will the centipede be there on the day of resurection?"

"Do you want to play football or not?"

"Yay!"

I go to the football field, still holding my soda bottle. As we approach the football field, Setayesh slows down. Loqman is there. As we get closer, more boys pause to look at us. On the other side of the field, Loqman takes his shirt off and scores a goal. When he sees Setayesh, he screams, "Goal!" louder and louder. He does this every time he sees us. Loqman's voice is so loud that you can hear his scream from far, but nobody tells him he is being loud.

The football field, with its two tin football goals and the old ball that Ali Karimi, a national football player, once donated to the boys, is the most important part of our neighbourhood, and the boys enjoy playing there very much. The field is too big for my feet to measure; it is bigger than our house and Ali's store. The boys pour water on the ground to prevent the dust from getting in their throats. Their clothes are always covered in mud. There is mud on our clothes too.

The boys gather around Loqman, all happy as they hug him for the goal. I am happy too. I'm a fan of our neighbourhood team. But we are not allowed to watch their matches. Loqman comes our way and pulls his hair back. Setayesh is scared. I still don't know why we're not allowed to be here. Loqman frowns. All the boys are looking at us, not speaking a word. Loqman steps forward.

"Didn't I tell you not to come here?"

"She wanted to."

"So what? The football field is no place for girls… it's a place full of a bunch of guys being rude. Girls shouldn't be here."

"I wanted to," I say.

"You are so wrong; I've told you a hundred times not to come here. Setayesh, can you come over here for a second?"

Setayesh and Loqman start to walk away together. I follow them. Loqman raises his hand to slap me, but he doesn't.

"Stay here for a second. I need to talk to Setayesh."

I start crying. Sometimes it doesn't work as easily as I'd like it to.

"Shut up," Loqman says.

Setayesh looks at me and tells him, "But Sara cried and said, 'Let's go to the football field.' She likes football."

"Sara is wrong, and I've said it a hundred times, you have no right to be here. This is not a place for girls. Boys are rude here."

"Well, ask them to stop being rude!" Setayesh says. She runs over to me when she sees me crying.

"Hey, wait!" Loqman shouts.

Setayesh tells me to stop crying, that she'll be back soon. But I cry louder. Loqman keeps calling Setayesh. Setayesh doesn't know if she should hug me or go to him.

"If I tell you a secret, will you promise to stop crying?"

I stop crying.

"Loqman wants to marry me when we grow up."

"I already knew." I cry.

"Please don't cry. I'll be right back."

Setayesh kisses me. But I keep crying and hit her. Setayesh looks back and forth between me and Loqman, who is looking at her angrily.

"He's waiting for me. I'll be right back."

I keep on crying restlessly.

"I'll tell you a secret that you don't know about if you stop crying," she whispers to me.

"What secret?" I look at her.

"You already asked me about it today. You are a grown girl, but promise not to tell Maman, okay? So… Baba… and his friends… will you promise not to tell anyone?"

"Yes."

"They gather and start a brazier. Do you know what that is?"

"No."

"It's a little stove for drugs. I didn't know about it either, but Loqman says we'll find out when we grow up. I heard Maman telling our aunt that all men are the same. If we go near them, it makes them angry. Stop crying now."

I stop crying. Although I don't understand it, I am sure Setayesh has told me a real secret that she hasn't told anyone yet, so I stop crying. Setayesh and Loqman go behind the field. As they leave, the other boys throw rocks at me and laugh. I put the still-closed bottle of Canada Dry on the ground next to me. I go behind the field to find Setayesh but she's not there. Loqman isn't there either. I'm scared.

I keep on running.

They're not there.

I keep on running.

They're nowhere to be found. It's too hot. I'm thirsty. I want to drink water but my hands are sweaty. I rub them against my clothes. My plastic slippers are hot and my feet are burning. I move my headband back and forth like Setayesh does. Then I pull my braided hair back. That's how she pulls her hair back.

"Setayesh? Setayesh?"

They don't respond. They're not here. I'm alone. I'm scared. If I go, Loqman will yell at me, and Setayesh won't stop him. She'll just hug me, and then Loqman will hit her for spoiling me. That's it. But being hit is better than being alone. Setayesh hugging me or crying is way better than being alone behind a football field. I'm thirsty. My lips have cracks in them from dehydration. I lick my lips to make them wet again but three seconds later they're dry again. One…two… three… I can count to thirty-nine. I want cold water. I run to Uncle Moji's place where there is a free water fountain. It gives free drinking water, and that's why everyone likes him. Uncle Moji gives candy to all the children and grownups, and makes everyone happy.

"Uncle Moji?" I yell.

Uncle Moji has the only green garden in the

neighbourhood. There is a fountain there, a mulberry tree, and an apple tree. It's beautiful in the yard behind the building. There are some big pickle barrels in the garage and some carpentry tools. Uncle Moji is making a big table for his family. Everyone knows he is the first person in the neighbourhood to be able to afford a big wooden table. I look at the table, which is not complete yet. The grass is green in his backyard. No one else has grass in our neighbourhood. No one has shade either, but Uncle Moji—he has trees for that.

Uncle Moji's bicycle is right next to the door. He is the only person in the neighbourhood who has a bicycle, and he has taught all the kids how to ride it. He let the boys ride his bicycle all by themselves and picked which girls could ride the bicycle with him. He told the girls that only boys are allowed to ride bicycles and that they should not tell their parents that he let them ride with him. He said that he is the only man who lets us ride bicycles in the neighbourhood.

I remember crying, telling him that I wanted to ride it alone, and then pushing him. He told me that I was very courageous but he couldn't let me ride alone as it's forbidden for girls. And now the bicycle is here, and there's nobody around to stop me. It is too big for me, and my feet can't reach the pedals. I stumble and fall down. I get up to try again but hear a voice.

"Uncle Moji?"

Nobody answers me. I'm alone. I hold my hands

under the fountain to drink cold water. I rub my wet hands on my face and arms to cool down a little, but I get hot again. After that, I go past the water fountain and the building, toward the big tree in Uncle Moji's yard. That's when I hear them. Loqman and Setayesh are sitting in the empty playground behind Uncle Moji's house.

Loqman says, "Let's play doctor."

I've seen this game a few times. Loqman becomes the doctor and examines Setayesh as she coughs. He puts his hand under her shirt and asks Setayesh to cough, then hits her chest and says, "Your lungs are very sick. I'll prescribe you some syrup."

Setayesh shakes a bit and drops her head. "I don't want to play doctor, I'm too ashamed."

"Oh baby," Loqman says.

"Why do you talk like a grownup?"

"Because I'm all grown and you're my wife."

"Let's play husband and wife."

"How do you play that game?" Loqman asks.

"You become my husband, go out and make money, come home, and scream that you're tired. I'll make you tea, cook food, and all that stuff." Setayesh pulls her hair back. I love it when she does that. She does it beautifully. I also pull my hair aside.

"Now that you're my wife, will you give me a kiss?" Loqman brings his face closer to hers.

Setayesh closes her eyes and shakes her head.

"It's okay if you kiss me. I want to marry you when I grow up, and you shouldn't kiss strangers."

Setayesh says, "Nope."

"You're not going to play doctor anymore?"

"Let's play husband and wife, and Sara will be our daughter. I'm going to get her."

"Can't we play doctor for a bit and then bring Sara to become our daughter?" Loqman takes her hand.

"No, we're going to play with Sara first, and then play doctor. Sara gets mad and cries when she's alone."

"You've become so cheeky. You just do whatever you want. You don't listen to me. Get lost. I don't want you anymore."

"I'm sorry. Let's play doctor and then husband and wife," Setayesh cries.

"If you want to become my wife, you'll do as I say."

"I'm sorry."

"Stop crying." He hugs her and kisses her head. He's a bit taller than her. "Give me a kiss."

She kisses his cheek as she cries.

"A good kiss, like they do in the movies." They press their lips together and Setayesh runs over to the swing. He goes after her. "Good! And don't you ever come to the football field again looking for your husband, it's not the place for you."

Setayesh sits on the swing and pulls her hair back. "Push me."

Loqman pushes her on the swing and she laughs.

Her skirt goes up, and her underpants are visible. She laughs. He pushes her harder and her skirt goes up even more. Loqman bends his head to see her underpants from under the swing. She laughs.

"You're my beautiful wife," Loqman says.

She laughs and he keeps pushing the swing. It looks like Loqman has to pee. I have to pee too. His eyes are half closed. Setayesh, on the other hand, with her hair in the wind, laughs and says, "Higher higher…"

He pushes the swing harder.

"It's very good." She keeps laughing.

"Higher!"

Loqman laughs and breathes faster as he pushes the swing harder. Every time Setayesh's skirt flies in the air, the wind blows it to one side and her underpants become visible. She giggles and doesn't even realize.

"Higher…"

Setayesh's screaming and laughing gets louder, and her face turns purple from the laughter, and tears stream out of her eyes. Loqman laughs and pushes the swing harder. He is not very strong. He breathes rapidly.

"You want it higher, right?"

"High enough to make me reach the sky."

The swing goes high up. She stretches her legs to reach the clouds, but there's still a long way to the clouds.

"Do your best. Higher, harder."

Loqman tries his best to push the swing harder so that it goes higher and higher. So high that Setayesh will see how strong he is, like no other boy in town. As if Setayesh is the queen of the world and only the best and strongest boy in town can push her swing. They laugh and cheer.

But I'm scared. I'm scared of the wind that moves Setayesh's hair from side to side and blows her skirt in the air. I'm scared that Setayesh's laughter reaches the sky even though her legs don't. I'm scared of how Loqman is peeing his pants and trying so hard to push the swing harder, sweating, and breathing rapidly. The sounds of Setayesh's laughter and screams are mixed up with Loqman's laughter and the squeak of the swing. Squeaking… breathing… laughter, screaming. They're so loud that even the clouds hear them and move away. It's like they're alone in this world. The whole world stops so that their voices fill up the air. Nothing makes a sound. The sparrows are silent. The tree branches aren't moving. Time has stopped.

I have to pee so badly that I can't stand up anymore. I get up to go to the bathroom, and I see Uncle Moji watching them from behind the tree. I feel scared. I have to pee. But I can't go to the bathroom, and I can't go toward Setayesh either. I can't even scream, "Uncle Moji is watching you swing!"

Setayesh and Loqman get really loud. Uncle Moji is watching with his eyes wide open and is waiting behind the tree to attack them. Just like a wild cat hunting a sparrow. They're so loud that I cover my ears. I hold my body tight so that I won't pee myself.

"What the hell are you doing, little bastards?" Uncle Moji finally comes out.

Loqman runs away as soon as he sees Uncle Moji, but Uncle Moji catches Loqman and hits him.

"What the hell were you doing? How old are you, kid?"

"I'm sorry sir, I'm twelve."

"Shut up, I'm gonna show you how to play doctor." He slaps him in the face. He pushes Loqman to the ground and kicks him. Loqman escapes. Setayesh is still on the swing, confused. She is wandering somewhere between the ground and the sky. She still doesn't know what's going on. Uncle Moji turns to Setayesh. She screams. He holds the swing and grabs Setayesh, "How old are you, huh?"

"Nine."

"Ah, so you've reached the age of majority."

Setayesh starts crying and screaming and shaking her limbs. I pee myself, and the pee moves down my legs and gets into my slippers. I want to cry, but I can't. I can't scream either. I'm disgusted by the pee on my legs. My slippers are soaked, and my feet slip in them.

Setayesh screams and Uncle holds her mouth. He wraps his arms tightly around Setayesh. She sees me standing behind the wall and stares as he drags her away. She is begging me with her eyes to come save her. But I can't move. She looks red and can't breathe.

Uncle Moji says, "You're filthy, I should wash you off with acid to make the filth go away!" He pulls Setayesh into the house. The same place Baba and his friends get medicine. The same place he gives us candy every time we come here with Baba to get medicine, and we eat candy until nighttime when Baba has guests. Baba always prays for Uncle Moji for his kindness. He gives candy to kids, he has a free drinking fountain, and he helps his neighbours. Setayesh gives me one last begging look.

One-two-two-two-three-four-five-six-seven-eight-nine-ten-eleven-twelve-twelve-thirteen-fourteen-fifteen-sixteen-seventeen-eighteen-nineteen-twenty-twenty-one-twenty-two-twenty-three-twenty-four-twenty-five-twenty-six-twenty-sevvvven-twenty-nineeee-thirty-seven-thirty-eight-thirty-thirty by thirty-nine…What comes after thirty-nine? What is next? That is as far as we've learned in school. I don't know how to count further.

2

SETAYESH HASN'T COME back home. Setayesh hasn't come home, and everybody is looking for her.

Setayesh is lost. Her photo is in all the newspapers and even in Ali's store: "A nine-year-old girl who left the house in perfect health and never returned!" In the photo, Setayesh wears a red-and-white overcoat, laughing as her bangs sweep across her face. I can hear her laughing in the picture.

I know where she is. Not exactly, but I know the last person to see her.

"Sara, darling, where is Setayesh?" Maman asks while crying.

I look at Maman and say, "Maman! Setayesh and Loqman were playing doctor, and then they went on the swings. Uncle Moji came and hit Loqman and took Setayesh with him. She was moving and crying

30

and even looked at me begging me to save her, but she left on Uncle Moji's shoulder. He said that she was filthy and that he should wash her off with acid. He then took Setayesh, and I heard her cry."

Maman smacks her head. "Why doesn't she talk?"

I repeat myself: "Maman! Setayesh and Loqman were playing doctor, and then the swing. Uncle Moji came and hit Loqman and took Setayesh with him. She was moving and crying and even looked at me begging me to save her, but she left on Uncle Moji's shoulder. He said that she was filthy and that he should wash her off with acid. He then took Setayesh, and I heard her cry."

Baba, with his face ashen, shakes me. "Sara, dear, why don't you say anything?"

And I repeat, again…

The doctor says, "This kid has been shocked and a part of her brain's natural process has been impaired. Her stutter is so severe that she is almost mute."

I can't get anything out of my throat, except for a few scattered noises. The image of Uncle Moji's thick mustache on Setayesh's face is always in my head. He's drooling. I watch Maman melt every day that Setayesh is missing. Baba smokes frequently, never saying a word. I don't feel like a kid at all, I feel like I've lived for many years. I have lived many years of suffering. I am an old woman.

I have no voice to speak and no tears to cry. For

days, we go to the temple to pray while Maman cries. As we pass through the crowd, I am the statue of a seven-year-old walking, staring into a faraway place, touching and kissing the tomb.

Maman says, "You should kiss the tomb. What the hell were you doing not seeing where Setayesh went? You should kiss the tomb and be thankful you didn't get lost instead!"

A neighbour says, "Kiss the tomb. You are a child — your heart is innocent. God will bring Setayesh back."

I don't have a voice, but my world is full of noises. Uncle Moji's, saying, "You're filthy. I should wash you off with acid." The squeak of the swing. Setayesh's laughter and Loqman's breathing. Setayesh's scream. The help she needed. *You're filthy!*

I am Setayesh too. If she is filthy, then I am filthy too. I'm probably bad too. Maman says, "You should thank God you didn't get lost." I hear people wish I was lost instead of Setayesh.

I wish I didn't exist. I wish I could get lost.

I'm bad! I couldn't bring Setayesh back home.

I'm bad. I couldn't open my mouth and say I saw her last on the swing with Loqman, and on Uncle Moji's shoulder when she was crying.

I'm bad. I couldn't respond to Setayesh's last begging look.

I'm bad. I shouldn't pee myself. I'm filthy and disgusting.

I don't speak. I just look at everybody. I can't say anything.

Loqman is there too, among the people who watch this disaster. But he just bends his head and walks away every time he sees me. If Loqman, who is stronger and older than me, is afraid to talk and say that Uncle Moji was the last person to have seen her, how can I?

Even Uncle Moji comes over every once in a while to get the news. "Haven't you found her? Where has this girl gone? What if she was mad at you and has run away from home? What did you do to this girl?"

I stare at the hair on Uncle Moji's arms stuck together from the heat, and I hear Setayesh scream. "Sara! Help!" I wet myself again. Whenever Uncle Moji looks at me, I press my legs together and tighten my body, and then dark! I don't remember a thing. I think to myself, the world is such an unsafe place! How is it possible to have lived for all these years already? I wish to stop existing.

Setayesh is gone. The grownups say she has been gone for a week now. She isn't here for me to hold her hand and cross the street, play with dolls, or play with her as Loqman's child. She's not here to point to Loqman and say, "Here's your baba!" And for me to imagine the coat hanger as Loqman and say, "Okay, he's my baba!" If she were here, she would wear Maman's white scarf and kiss the hanger and say, "Loqman and my wedding!" She would then push me and say, "You can't be at our wedding, my child." "Where was I? In your belly?" And Setayesh would say, "No, not even in my belly. Your father and I will get married first, and then kiss in front of everybody, and pray to God for you. God will accept our prayers and put you in my belly. Then the doctors will tear my belly open and bring you out, and then stitch up my belly. Loqman and I will raise you." Whenever I imagine that, I wish not to exist until the day Setayesh and Loqman get married. This time, I would get out of Setayesh's belly instead of Maman's, and be her child.

Everybody is looking at me.

A police car is here with some detectives. The police car blocks our narrow alley. A police officer is sitting right in front of me.

"Dear Sara, on the day you were playing, kids say Setayesh and Loqman went away. Did you see them?"

"Yes, I did. Loqman kissed Setayesh, and she got on the swing, the wind made her underpants visible. Uncle Moji was watching them, just like me, and he hit Loqman, then said, 'Setayesh, haven't you reached the age of majority yet?' And then he took her and told her she was filthy."

The officer says, "I know you can't speak, so just nod or shake your head. Did you see them? Yes or no?"

I look at him.

All the boys from the soccer game are here. They tell the police officer that I followed Setayesh and Loqman behind the football field. The police officer looks at me, and I see Loqman, who is crying, coming over with another officer. His baba hits his head a couple of times. I look at him.

For a moment I feel like he's talking to me: *Setayesh, give me a kiss, just like in the movies! It's okay if you kiss me. I want to marry you when I grow up, and you shouldn't kiss others.* I say, *Nope.* And as I touch my hair to pull it, I realize my hair isn't that long. I'm not Setayesh! I stop. I will never touch my hair again, nor will I close my eyes to pull my hair aside.

"I swear to God I haven't seen her," Loqman cries.

His baba hits him again. He cries and says, "I just took her behind the field and told her 'You shouldn't be there with the boys' and 'You have reached the age of majority, what is that skirt you're wearing? Where is your scarf?' And then Sara came and they took off, I promise."

Everybody turns around and looks at me.

"She knows, ask her," he says.

We look at each other. Through his eyes, it feels like he's saying: "I'm scared, Setayesh. What do you expect from me?"

My parents come toward me. "Sara. Your sister is lost. Tell us where she is. Say something, or at least nod…"

Baba shakes me. I just watch as Loqman and his father go home.

"It's all your fault," Baba says to Maman. "Why did you kick them out?"

"What could I do? Let them watch you and your friends smoke?"

"It would have been better than this."

"The last time, Setayesh was just a baby when she burned her legs on your brazier."

"Still, you should have been patient and not kicked them out."

"If you were man enough, you wouldn't start a brazier for opium in front of your wife and kids every day."

"What?"

"Nothing."

"What did you say to your husband?"

"Nothing, I'm sorry."

My left leg burns. I put my hand under my skirt and touch a bump on my leg. So, they burned Setayesh's leg, and that's why she got scared every time we had guests, and took my hand and left the house.

"Hold on a minute," says the police officer. "Now is not the right time for this conversation." He steps closer. "Darling, where did you and Setayesh go next? Did you go somewhere after Loqman left?"

Uncle Moji enters our house in pajamas and slippers, and sees the officer. As he gets closer, I tighten my body. I hold it. I keep telling myself: I'm not gonna pee, I'm not gonna pee, I'm not gonna pee…

3

AT HOME, I WALK BY THE mirror. I look at it, and it looks back. Is this me? How is this me? I'm so old. How can I have lived this much? I have the face of a child but a soul that fits more wounds every day. I push aside my skirt. The scar that was on Setayesh's left leg ever since she was an infant is now on my leg. I want to ask Maman whether her scar was on the left or right side of the leg. But I can't ask anyone anything. I have no right to ask questions.

During the second week since Setayesh's disappearance, all the neighbours gather in front of our house and mourn, each one louder than the next.

Maman listens to them all and then says, "I heard Setayesh's voice. She laughed and her voice echoed in the house. She said, 'Maman? Baba? Sara, where are you? I went to play near Uncle Moji's house. I'm sorry I forgot to tell you. It was so much fun that I forgot to come back home. Why are all the neighbours here? Why is everybody sad?' She then giggled and hugged me. She pulled her hair back and told me: 'I'm back! Be happy!'"

All the neighbours shed tears of joy and say, "What a great dream, Suossan. It's a blessing. She will be found. Maybe she really went to play and got lost. Your dream will have a positive outcome."

After hearing Maman's dream, I am more confident than ever that Setayesh will never come back. I know she does not exist in this world anymore. I know she is gone. Setayesh is part of me now, and I feel Uncle Moji's hairy face on my face. His sweaty arms. Uncle Moji holds me and I kick him. He takes me home and hits my legs with a stick, and tells me, "Open your legs you filthy slut! You should be washed off with acid."

He bites my legs and demands, "You show your underpants and flirt with a stranger?"

I do not know what either *flirt* or *stranger* mean. I yell. "Sara! Help!"

"Shut up! Stop yelling!" says Uncle Moji, covering my mouth.

I am breathless. I know where Setayesh is. She is in a dark place. A very dark place. I know she is in a dark place that smells like acid. I am about to live there forever, too.

The phone rings. One of the neighbours answers and then calls for Maman. "Suossan, my husband is calling from the forensic medicine centre, and he says a few young girls have been found. Does Setayesh have any unique features?"

"Ey Vaay!" Maman sits on her knees. "A nine-year-old with long hair and black eyes, and a scar from a burn on her left leg."

Time moves so slowly. She is talking about my scar, on my left leg. All the noises have mixed together, and I see Baba's friends placing hot charcoal on my leg and telling me to leave and not interrupt their pleasure. I feel pangs in the bone in my left leg, and my skin stretching. My whole body is in pain.

After passing along the description, the neighbour finally expresses relief and hangs up the phone. "She is probably alive and is just lost then. No news is good news. If anything had happened, she would be at the forensic medicine centre."

Everybody says prayers. Hope has found its way back. Maman can stand up again. She laughs.

I want to scream, with my nonexistent voice, "Hey! People! She's not coming back."

4

I'M SITTING BY THE DOOR in our earthy, narrow alleyway. Samaneh and her friends are playing, but Setayesh is not with them. Samaneh looks at me and asks me to come play. "We won't make fun of you for being little. I'm sorry we made fun of you earlier. Sara, come play with us. We have one person missing." She hugs me.

I see Setayesh laughing and playing with them. Her skirt moving as she jumps up and down. I look at Samaneh. I know she misses Setayesh. I miss her too. My slipper slips off my foot, and I bend over to pick it up. When I get back up Uncle Moji is standing behind me. We both stand there, staring at each other.

"Come over here," he says. He picks up a stick and hits my leg with it. "What is that you're wearing? And it goes up when you bend over."

I say to myself: I'm not gonna pee, I'm not gonna pee, I'm not gonna pee…

"I'm not going to hurt you." He shows me a piece of candy.

I just tighten myself up and say to myself, *I don't have to pee.* I can't control my pee. "I don't have to pee," I say. After seventeen days, I finally have my voice back. I scream. "It was Uncle Moji! He took Setayesh away on his shoulder!"

I'm screaming, but I don't know if anyone can hear me. I'm counting to thirty-nine in my head, and then there's that acidic smell and the dark.

When I finally open my eyes again, there is absolute darkness. I can hear sounds, but my vision is blurry. It takes a while to be able to see clearly. Everybody is talking, crying. I have no idea what's happened. Then I hear someone say that Uncle Moji is under arrest.

After that, everything becomes worse. Everyone is more confused than before. Maman doesn't know what to do anymore. She keeps on hitting herself. Baba feels more broken and uses more opium. If Setayesh were here, she would probably tell me, "Hush, don't say a word to anyone about it, but all the men have gathered around the brazier."

Maman says, "He was right in front of us, and we didn't realize."

Everybody has heard the news. They've all gathered in front of our house. The police say, "We guess that Sara has been assaulted too and that's why she is shocked and silent."

"Ey Vaay!" Maman hits herself harder.

Maman kisses Ms. Bibi's hands. Our neighbour Ms. Bibi was the first to notice that I couldn't control my pee when I was around Uncle Moji, the way he looked at me that day when I bent over. Ms. Bibi was the one who heard me scream in the alleyway when Uncle Moji came near me. She realized I was different with Uncle Moji after Setayesh disappeared, and she put together all her suspicions and reported them to the police.

And now Uncle Moji is a suspect for murder. Loqman and other girls have started speaking up too. Others are still silent and not reporting the rape of their daughters, for the sake of reputation. The whole neighbourhood is mourning. The newspapers and the whole town know. They're all talking about Setayesh.

The police have searched Uncle Moji's house but haven't found evidence. I want to tell them to search the dark place with the acidic smell. But nobody can hear me again. They've been looking for her body for two days. Eventually, Uncle Moji starts crying and says he regrets what happened and he didn't want to kill or even assault Setayesh, but that she was seductive and turned him on. He said that he wanted to guide her in the right direction so as to not play doctor with strangers, but then Setayesh moved her skirt aside and seduced him.

"Disgusting man! You should be ashamed! She was just a child!" the neighbours say.

Uncle Moji confesses where the body is: in the backyard inside a barrel of pickles. He says he regrets everything and that he only did it to prevent sin and obey God's command, but he didn't want things to end up this way.

The police search the house. They find pieces of my sister's body in the pickle barrel.

That's how cruel this is! It's so hard putting those words together: "pieces of my sister!" My blood is cold. The warm and fresh blood of a child cannot say "pieces of my sister!"

It's in the newspapers. Uncle Moji admitted his regret after arrest, but now he claims that this was the right punishment for a girl who has reached the age of majority but doesn't wear a hijab. He says he didn't mean to kill her, but she kept on screaming, "Maman! Baba! Sara!" It made Uncle Moji cover her mouth, which led to her death without him noticing it.

The people of Tehran are filled with hatred, and they all want retribution. "He wanted to punish her for wearing short skirts and playing with a strange boy, which got him here! We ask all families to be cautious regarding their young girls."

But it's different for me. I have lost my sister. These people have only heard about the dark and the acidic smell, but all these nights I've felt it, in my dreams or

wide awake. Eternal darkness, pickle barrels and me –
we're attached. They have sent me to a dark room and
I wonder if, one day, a window will ever open for me.

And now, maybe all the little girls know why Uncle
Moji was the only person who would let them ride his
bicycle with him and ask them not to tell their parents
about it.

I whisper, "pieces of my sister!" I say it in cold blood.

5

MY MOTHER CAN'T STAND bad news, so she has asked Ms. Bibi and Ms. Soheila to take me for a check-up. The hospital is in an asphalted region, filled with buses and cars, unlike our neighbourhood, which is made of dirt. The people here are prettier. The square in front of the hospital building is even bigger than the football field in our neighbourhood.

A young girl and two women are waiting before me. They do not look at us at all. The girl cries. She doesn't want to go in. I get scared. She is much older than me and she still doesn't want to go in. This is probably a bad place. I tense up and hold Ms. Bibi.

When the doctors call her in, the women who are with her push her into a closed room.

"You have no right to do this!" the girl cries.

"We don't even know what the hell she's done for her to be so scared," says one woman to the people in the waiting room, as the other woman pushes her inside.

Ms. Bibi and Ms. Soheila look at each other. "She's her future mother-in-law," Ms. Soheila says.

"Well, she has the right to know," Ms. Bibi nods.

The girl's scarf falls down as she tries to escape. She keeps on screaming and finally she escapes. She runs around the waiting area screaming, "I didn't do anything! You have no right to do this!"

"Shut up!" the mother-in-law shouts. "If you were innocent, you wouldn't cause so much drama!"

"Even your own son disagrees with you," the girl says. "But he's scared of you!"

"Then why are you running away?" the other woman yells.

The girl runs down the hall and disappears.

Two of the nurses apologize. "We get a lot of these people here."

"Yes, exactly!" nod the two women who brought the girl in. "It's better that we find out before she gets married."

Then it's our turn. Soheila and Bibi hold my hand and take me into the room. Bibi keeps talking to me so that I don't hear the women arguing outside. Inside, there is a curtain and a bed by the doctor's desk. The doctor asks me to sit on the bed. Soheila picks me up and puts me on it.

The doctor comes closer. I can smell that she's a woman, a strange smell that's so familiar. I also smell alcohol and fear, doctors and hospitals.

"Oh wow, is this her?" says the doctor. "May God bless her mother with patience. Sit here, darling. What a pretty girl with pretty hair."

I reach for my hair to pull it out, but I stop. I don't touch my hair. I have to be careful. Ms. Bibi and Ms. Soheila look at each other, and the doctor looks at them.

"Darling, are you okay? Do you want chocolate?" asks the doctor.

I want chocolate but I don't say a word.

"At least nod."

I don't!

It's like everything's suddenly changing in me. It's like I now know a lot of things I had no idea about just a few minutes ago. Being in such a place at this age means I have passed through many years. This place is not a hospital, even though there is a doctor. It's a place where they make choices for you and your life, and decide whether you're a good girl or not. This place smells like all the women in history who were ever judged. All the women who were ever scared. All the women who were ever called corrupt or sinful. This place smells like women.

The doctor takes my clothes off. I twist and scream. Nurses hold me in place. Just like Setayesh. Just like the

47

girl before me. The doctor and the nurses are strong. The doctor lets go of me, and I stop screaming, but all of my muscles are tight, and I have to pee. I keep telling myself: I'm not gonna pee, I'm not gonna pee.

"I hope this girl is healthy, I will walk to Karbala if she is." Ms. Bibi prays to Imam Hussein.

The doctor smiles with satisfaction. "Thank God Setayesh's sister has not been assaulted!"

She must be joking! Who gave her the power to be a doctor? I know how many times I've been assaulted. At this moment, as I'm being judged, I see a force within myself, the old lady I will become and have always been, who orders me to be silent as she pushes away my seven-year-old self. She wants to rule my body and soul. I am not seven years old anymore. I haven't been seven for a few days now. I can feel it. I am one hundred and fourteen years old. I want to scream and tell them that I have been assaulted, not once but many times throughout my lifetime. How can this lady, with all her experience, sit here and say, "Thank God she has not been assaulted!" Why should she decide whether I've been assaulted or not when I myself can recall the entire one-hundred-and-fourteen-year history of who assaulted me and where? I admit, with my silent voice: "I've been assaulted." I want to scream so loud and make the whole building crash down on their heads. I want my scream to ruin their everything. To take revenge for Setayesh and that girl before me, and all the girls before

48

me. The doctor offers me another chocolate, and I push it away with my hand, and all the chocolates fall to the floor.

6

The day of execution!

Execution of the murderer.

Execution of Uncle Moji the murderer.

This day feels like the day of resurrection, with my mother's whimpers and the sinner getting the merit of his sin. The day of resurrection cannot be any worse than this. A qualified Muslim judge has decided that Uncle Moji's life must be taken in return for taking someone's life. A judge in Islam is God's representative on Earth, and the first requirement is that he must be a man. My parents have asked the judge for the greatest punishment. Uncle Moji is about to die.

I want to open my mouth and say, "He'll go where Setayesh is if he dies. Don't kill him. For years to come, he must suffer the way Setayesh did during her last minutes.

One hundred and fourteen years of imprisonment. One hundred and fourteen years in a pickle barrel. This is the best revenge." I know Setayesh will cry when she sees him again, just like the day she needed help.

Bibi says Setayesh has gone to Heaven and Uncle Moji will be punished for his sins by being sent to Hell. *Execution, rape, punishment for sins, the greatest punishment, court—these are the words that keep ringing in my ears.* Here in the middle of the town square, somewhere near our house in our dirt neighbourhood, everyone has gathered to observe the execution of Uncle Moji the rapist murderer. Is the moment a murderer dies any different than others? Maybe their conscience wraps around their whole existence and the resentment is released at the moment of death.

"Why does this have to be a lesson for us poor people?" our neighbour Soheila shouts at the crowd. "Why don't rich people put on these types of shows? They never do this in rich areas, maybe because they have other entertainment. Or maybe because if they do that in their areas, people will protest. Maybe because they think that they deserve a better life and they are rich and spoiled."

The others silence her.

"He must be killed right before our eyes," Baba shouts. "For the sake of my revenge for my daughter's blood!"

Soheila stops talking, and the crowd keeps cheering.

We are killing the killer. The place smells like sweat and hatred. The air is heavy.

The crowd shouts: "The execution crane is here!" A man explains to his son, who is about my age, how the construction crane lifts the murderer and how he dies. The young boy looks at me. It's as if all the male victims in history live in him. He looks at me as if he knows at the end of this story there's neither more security nor lessons for others, nor any relief for one's pain. We look at each other.

I can hear reporters taking photos. I can hear security guards encouraging people to calm down, asking them to stay behind the fences. We are all behind the fences. A few police cars arrive. The young boy knows that I and all the women in history are here. I know that he and all the men in history are here too. It is so crowded that we lose each other.

The Quran blasts through the speakers. It calms me down. Whenever I hear the Quran, I know this world has a mother and we are not orphans here. The smell of the Quran is rosewater. I don't know why. Maybe it is for rosewater everywhere the Quran is played, like the mosque. I can smell rosewater.

We are getting crushed among the crowd. I feel pain. Everybody is pushing against one another. Some are sad that they can't see anything. The crane operator prepares to raise the crane. You can hear all accusations against Uncle Moji through the speakers. "Moji, son of so-and-so, father of so-and-so, husband of so-and-so…" You cannot smell the rosewater anymore. It smells like fear now. You can hear people scream. "Allah-u-Akbar, Allah-u-Akbar, Allah-u-Akbar," you hear through the loudspeakers. "To the zealous and martyr-loving people, pay attention! The death sentence against the aggressor is now being executed! For it should be a lesson for those who fight God on Earth! Allah-u-Akbar! God is the greatest!" Everyone has their phones and cameras out to take videos. I am being crushed.

Finally, Uncle Moji is brought out. Baba picks me up on his shoulders to watch Uncle Moji receive the punishment. Baba used to pick Setayesh and me up and put us both on his shoulders. He would become our donkey, and we would play while on his shoulders. But it's been so long since Baba has done that. If Setayesh could see us like this right now, she would pull Baba's shirt and say, "It's my turn."

I see everything from up there. I see Uncle Moji blindfolded and his hands tied! From up here, I can see the ring on his finger. I can smell fear, humanity's fear of itself. That's why people find joy in watching others being tortured, because they know their turn has been postponed. We're here to see Uncle Moji's guilty conscience end too soon with death. This is not justice for Uncle Moji, but justice for the people watching here today, or even justice for people who hate him. Watching the execution take place is justice for the people who watch.

The moment Uncle Moji takes his last breath, Maman will feel relieved. All the other women shout, "You deserve it. Jerk!" Maman and Baba breathe deeply. They scream. They feel a sense of satisfaction.

Maman thinks she'll feel relieved. But from this moment on, this will be a punishment for all of us. Nobody understands this. Only I, by traveling back in time one hundred and seven years and going back to the prison of being seven, can understand this. Uncle Moji will soon leave this world and suffer no more, while our hatred of him will live with us forever. As we watch him die, his shaking will shake our souls forever. We feel ashamed of all the assaults we commit every day, so we run away from ourselves and try to cover up our sins by blaming them on others.

Uncle Moji should stay alive. He must spend the rest of his life in solitary confinement, alone with his conscience. The days of his life must be multiplied by one thousand and go on forever. But the law and the judge believe in a life for a life!

This is just like the day of resurrection for the people who have come here with their children. They've come here to prosecute their own dark sides—the disgusting side they all try to run away from their whole lives, even though it keeps chasing them like a shadow. I who am one hundred and fourteen knows that there's no such thing as a decent human being. Human beings live always in ignorance and are destined to make peace with the dark side they've inherited from their ancestors.

The crane operator pulls Uncle Moji up as the guards remove the floorboards from under his feet. He shakes as the crowd screams, "Hurray!"

After he's done shaking, we know he's done. Everybody makes noise. Maman moans at the top of her lungs. The whole place is noisy, but as I watch from on top of Baba's shoulders, I know this is the moment everybody should be silent and look deep within themselves. I see people cursing and throwing stones at Uncle Moji. Kids my age scream. "Hurray!"

I see Uncle Moji's daughter watching her baba die, Uncle Moji's mother crying and hitting herself, and my mother crying, the tracks of her fingernails still visible on her face. When a disaster takes place, it doesn't matter who's the victim and who's watching, who's the criminal and who's the prosecutor. Everyone is a victim, a bunch of sinners to feel sorry for, somehow everyone is guilty regardless of how big or small their sins are.

Baba has become so skinny that the bones of his shoulder sink into my body. There's nothing left of him. Setayesh's presence is everywhere but nowhere. Death has conquered everyone here today.

I miss Setayesh. I want to hold her hand, I just want her to close her eyes and pull her hair back once again. I want to go out with her and play!

The crane operator raises Uncle Moji's body up high so that the whole neighbourhood can see him, feel relieved, and learn a lesson about thinking twice before attempting an assault.

"Sara, dear, watch the death of your sister's murderer closely," Baba says. "Can you feel the relief?"

I watch closely. Every second of it makes me feel hatred. Hatred for him, people, Maman, Baba, myself, the world. A world that takes Setayesh from us like that is certainly a bad place. With my eyes full of hatred, I watch closely as Uncle Moji dies.

I hate this horrible day.

I hate the shadow under the tree in Uncle Moji's yard.

I hate the crowd and how they shout, "Hurray!"

I hate the squeaking of the swing, sunlight and thirst, glasses of cold water.

I hate football, playing husband and wife, playing doctor, Loqman.

I see Loqman in the crowd shouting, "Hurray!" I look at him, directly, with hatred. He becomes silent when he sees me. Uncle Moji's mother is still crying, as are his family and my parents.

I hate everyone.

7

In the autumn of that same year, I go to school.

The school is so huge that I can't measure it with my feet. It is so big and crowded it makes me sick to measure it with my feet. The school is full of girls wearing scarves. All the girls wear pink coats with white scarves. Everybody's doing something. Some play. Some laugh. Some eat snacks. Some fight. And some rehearse revolutionary anthems. On the wall, there are paintings of women in hijabs.

On the first day, Maman says something to my teacher by the classroom door. The teacher looks at me. Maman leaves. The class is full of young girls. We sit three girls to one bench. The desks are old, and they're engraved with mementos.

"It is the first day of school for you," says the teacher. "Tomorrow all the other children will start school, but you are here a day early because you're first graders and you need to familiarize yourselves with school and learn how to be responsible for yourselves."

"What does it mean to be responsible for yourself?" the students ask.

"Who knows what it means?" the teacher asks.

I raise my hand. Everybody looks at me. I have been hearing about it for one hundred and fourteen years, how could I not know what it means?

"Can you tell everyone what it means?"

I am silent.

She repeats her question. I remain silent.

"She's lying," all the children laugh. "She doesn't know!"

I remain silent.

"Come whisper it to me," says the teacher.

I remain silent.

The teacher pauses for a second, like she just remembered what Maman had told her. "Okay, let's read the attendance list." She goes back to her desk and picks up a paper.

"Parvin?"

"Present!"

"Qamar?"

"Present!"

"Forooq?"

"Present!"

"Maryam?"

"Present!"

"Shahrnoosh?"

"Present!"

"Shirin?"

"Present!"

"Goli?"

"Present!"

She calls all the names but mine. "She didn't call your name," says the girl next to me.

I remain silent.

"Excuse me, Madame. You didn't call her name!"

"I know, I checked her present."

I wish the teacher hadn't said that!

At the break, as the teacher steps out of the class, the tallest girl in class comes up to me. "I'm Raana. These are Neda, Shima, and Maryam. What's your name?"

I remain silent.

"Hey, I'm talking to you. Are you deaf?"

I remain silent.

"Cheeky girl looks at me, but doesn't answer me."

I remain silent. I take my scarf off and show them my frizzy hair that I haven't brushed since Setayesh's death.

"Look at her hair!" The kids laugh. They throw my scarf around, poke me and laugh. They all laugh, clap and say "hurray!" just like the day of resurrection. They make fun of my frizzy hair.

I remain silent, my body tightened, my head down. Uncle Moji was also tense, his head down when people said, "Hurray!" I raise my hand to pull my hair back, but I can't move. I put my hands down. My body is stiff. I'm not gonna pee, I'm not gonna pee, I'm not gonna pee. This whole time in school, I am the old woman stuck with children. They think I'm deaf, and maybe a bit slow, but I am an old woman in the body of a child, unable to speak. Speech is my weakness. I don't have a voice. When the kids take my scarf and make fun of me, I remain silent. This is how cruel people treat others when they themselves are weak.

When I get home, I pass the mirror. I never look in the mirror, but today something unusual catches my eye. The old woman has done her deed, and after the kids have thrown my scarf around, she has manifested. The pressure of this day is an alibi for her to show herself off. I look at my hair. It is all white. I don't know why I feel indifferent. It's as though I have already seen myself like this many times.

In the following weeks at school, the teachers try to make me utter any word, using a lot of tricks. Sometimes I can barely speak a few words like, "Myyy name iiis Saaaraaaa." Or, "I'm eeeighttt." Sometimes I try so hard to move my tongue, but it doesn't happen, it's locked, it doesn't move. I feel warm, but my tongue doesn't warm up. The teachers try very hard to make me say those words, and the kids keep on laughing.

I am the only old woman in school. Who else can say their hair went white overnight? I can wear a veil and escape school to go to the mosque. The mosque and the veil protect me from the evil of people. The mosque for me is a shelter where I'm not afraid of anything. I don't have to talk to anybody or show my hair. It is the only place that respects my most comfortable self.

That's how I become a religious woman after Setayesh's murder, more religious than my aunts, more religious than the collective subconscious of the women of my country, even more than the women who narrate religious stories. In a world where love is not enough, religion is my everything. The only thing giving me a sense of identity and existence is reaching out to the sky. When no one wants anything to do with me, I look out for myself.

I don't know if it is good luck or bad luck to be this old and speechless at such a young age, to have such an empty life and to therefore be so weak as to let religion take over my life, fill in the place of my nonexistent friends, and heal the wounds of years of pain and missing my sister.

As I get older, I memorize more Surahs of the Quran. Sometimes I get so caught up in my imagination that I picture my future husband being the muezzin at the mosque I go to. The muezzin I have never met, whose voice touches my heart and makes me imagine what could be. When you don't speak, you listen. The muezzin's rough voice indicates a lack of confidence. But he wants to be the best. He tries to be the best muezzin in the world.

The Quran is a way to make all the noise in my head shut up. I am speechless but the voice inside me speaks all the time. Nobody but me can hear how much this brain talks, complaining and doubting nonstop. My brain hates everyone and has no love, caring only about its needs. My brain can stare at the blue ceiling of the mosque for hours and in its patterns create a better world for itself. A world in which good people go to Heaven and bad people go to Hell and justice is fair. In that world, Setayesh would go to Heaven and not see Uncle Moji, and he would get his punishment and not go to Heaven. In those circles on the ceiling, I see myself going to Heaven where Setayesh belongs, whenever I read more of the Quran. I have to go to Setayesh, and the only guarantee for going to Heaven is the Quran. This is what our theology teacher says.

The mosque is a bridge to Heaven, where all the innocent children await us, to welcome us when we die. The mosque is beautiful, and with its high ceiling full of signs from Heaven it belittles every human being in God's glory. Among the tiny flowers on the mosque's ceiling, I see all the women whose innocence takes them to Heaven. Innocence is the highest value of good. The tiny flowers indicate different degrees of Heaven. As

I read more of the Quran, I make for myself a bigger home in Heaven and plant more flowers in my eternal home. I pray to build my home where Setayesh is, just like the house on Jordan Street where Maman now works as a helper—a huge house with lots of flowers, in a beautiful neighbourhood with kind neighbours. That place is Heaven compared to our house and our neighbourhood.

8

A FEW MONTHS AFTER Setayesh was murdered, we needed money so our neighbour sent Maman as a helper to one of those uptown parties, a white house with a lot of trees. A yard with many trees is beautiful, like the one at the Shah's palace that we went to visit on a field trip with school. Heaven must be a place like the Shah's palace in Saadabad. Or in the yard of this house where Maman now serves as help.

It is a huge garden for a huge house. The house is almost as big as our whole neighbourhood, but it's cleaner, newer, and whiter. Even the neighbourhood is filled with trees and shade. Is this Tehran? Or is it another planet? I have heard that the neighbourhoods in the north of Tehran are clean and beautiful, but I never thought that the heaven I imagined could be in Tehran.

This house smells like perfume, a sweet scent. I don't

know what it is, but it's very pleasant. The hostess sees me smelling the air and says, "Do you like my perfume?"

She is wearing makeup, and she is beautifully dressed. She has a daughter my age called Natasha Nanushkai. Natasha and the rest of her family live in Canada, but are staying in their Tehran home for a visit.

Maman helps Natasha's mother in the kitchen, while we play in her parents' bedroom, where there is a very big bed between the vanity and the closet. I sit and watch her.

"Let's play a game that doesn't require speaking," says Natasha.

How kind she is. She knows that I am not able to communicate with her. Perhaps her maman told her. We pretend we're friends eating brunch.

"Do you know what brunch is?" she says. "It's like breakfast. And we'll go to the Old Port for coffee. Do you know where that is? Somewhere by the river in Montreal. You know where Montreal is, right? A city in Canada. We'll dress up like grownups, and I'll put on your makeup. We'll go out and talk about our kids in kindergarten. Okay?" She points to her maman's closet. "My mom has guests. She won't come in here today. Let's wear her lipstick."

As I sit there, I repeat to myself: Old Port, Montreal, Canada… Voices remain on Earth forever. They do not disappear. When you don't speak, you can hear better, even if it is to hear a woman from years ago.

Natasha paints my face. "I'll do your lipstick. Now close your eyes. A little bit of eye shadow and mascara. Okay, let's get some of my mom's clothes."

She is so comfortable and precise. It's like she's from another planet. I take a scarf from her maman's closet and look at her teetering in her oversized high-heeled shoes.

"What is that on your head?" she says. "They don't wear scarves in other countries."

Natasha pulls my scarf. "In foreign countries, grown-ups don't wear scarves, even outside. But look. They wear these shoes!"

The whole night, she talks about the strange planet she comes from, where grown women don't wear scarves when they go out. On this planet, everyone does! Maman, Soheila, Bibi, neighbours, all the women I see every day on the streets… everyone.

Soon after, I begin to hear voices in the other parts of the house, Natasha's maman comes into the bedroom and tells us it's time for kids to go to bed. The guests are arriving. She takes us to Natasha's room and tells us a bedtime story, the story of Arash the Archer, and how he had to determine the borders of Iran with his bow and arrow during the war with Turan. Arash the Archer spends the night thinking about how far he can throw the arrow for his country, and when he does so he puts his life on the line, and the arrow takes his life away. Days go by until the arrow hits the ground, where it becomes the border of Persia. Arash placed his soul, his entire life, into that arrow to make it fly farther and stretch the borders of Persia as far as possible. That's why Arash has become eternal in Persian history. I want to be like him. The smell of Natasha's maman's perfume mixes with the smell coming out of her mouth, which smells like the alcohol at the doctor's office at Ebn-e-Sina hospital, or like the scorpions and snakes that are kept in jars of alcohol at school.

Natasha goes to sleep, and I also close my eyes. When her maman leaves, I open my eyes and look at her room filled with Barbie dolls. The bedroom has a large window and a balcony full of flowers. I think about all the women I know who wear scarves when they go outside.

I hear music. More guests have arrived. It's foreign music. I get out of bed and look out at the living room from behind the door. It is dark, and women who don't have hijabs dance with men and drink colourful drinks without straws! They dress like nobody I know. The party is like the planet Natasha described. Maman walks around among the guests with her scarf on, cleans up their plates, and serves them food as people eat while dancing. Here, in uptown Tehran, people are not like us. Not like Bibi or neighbours, Maman or aunties, or even Setayesh, who is the prettiest girl in the whole world. They are like Natasha, Natasha Nanushkai!

A woman sees me and comes closer. "Honey, you need to go back to sleep, parties are not the place for children."

She bends over and I can see her breasts. One of the differences between this party and Baba's is that women are also here. At Baba's parties, women have to get out. The woman stumbles and a young man grabs her.

"Wow, I've had too much to drink!" she says. They both laugh.

I close the door, and the hallway gets dark, so dark that I can't see a thing. I feel along the walls to find Natasha's bedroom. In the bedroom, there's a night light on. Natasha is still asleep and I lie next to her. It's all like a dream. These people do not exist.

Maman wakes me up at midnight. Natasha's maman calls us a cab and gives Maman a bag full of hand-me-down clothes and some food. She pays for the cab and says to me, "What a pretty girl, you were such a good girl today. Come over again and play with Natasha."

Me? Pretty? No one has ever called me pretty. My Maman closes the door and the cab drives off.

"Sir, can you open the window?" Maman says, "The smell of drinks and cigarettes really bothered me."

"Well, it's a party," says the driver.

"You should have seen these women, smoking and drinking. These are bad times!"

The driver doesn't say anything.

I think that what these women from another

planet did is bad! We should always be good enough to be complimented all the time. That's what our teacher taught us!

Maman opens the window and the smell of uptown flowers fills the cab. The moon chases behind the car. If I were Arash the Archer, I would throw my arrow at the moon or a planet so that we could all be the same. So that all women would dress the same way and all houses would become villas full of flowers.

I travel to the future in my imagination. To the world on the beautiful ceiling of the mosque of the Heaven God promises, full of miniature blue flowers, where no man can slip in and sin. I stare at the ceiling for hours and pick flowers with Setayesh.

Everybody calls me the silent girl, but my world is full of noise. It's all noise. The voices of a million people crawling inside me. I am unimportant to everyone. I am invisible, but nobody hears the yelling inside me.

Driving in the taxi through Tehran, I see that Setayesh's picture is still all over the city and everybody still remembers her. I am nothing. I can only compete with Setayesh by getting closer to God. Setayesh, who was the symbol of innocence and purity, is still loved by the whole city almost a year later. Everybody says Setayesh has gone to Heaven, and I have to do whatever I can to go to Heaven too. I'll never show my hair again. There must be a shortcut to making that deal with God.

PART TWO

Defence

1

THE MOSQUE IS A PLACE where us Muslims pray and talk to God. In this beautiful place, the ground is covered with Persian carpets and we lie down and give thanks to God.

The mosque always smells like rosewater because we take our shoes off there and don't step on the carpet with our shoes on. Too many feet in this place can get smelly, so rosewater is used to make the mosque fragrant. Most people find the combination of the smells disgusting, but for me this is a place of salvation. I'm here and so is God, to protect me from all men.

From the women's section in the mosque, I can stare at the high ceiling. I can lie on the carpet. I can sleep. I can cry. I can read the Quran. I can reflect while staring at the heavenly miniature paintings on the ceiling. This is the only place where I can be myself and be free. To me, this is freedom. I don't care about the women in me, screaming that freedom is something different. The ceiling is high, so you can feel the greatness of the universe and the distance between Heaven and us.

Only the little boys who come to the mosque with their mamans have seen both the men and women's sides. Even though there is a curtain, I'm always tempted to pull it back and see what happens on the other side, in the men's world.

I now wear a loose veil to protect me from looks and a tight scarf underneath, stuck to my head. People can't see my white hair, and my hair doesn't get in my face like Setayesh's did. I have aged for all the years I haven't lived, and I know more about God than the old women in my family. I see women in tight clothes with their hair down, wearing lots of makeup, and I want to tell them what they're showing will get them into trouble one day. These are the flames of Hell. But it isn't possible. To them, I'm not a one-hundred-and-fourteen-year-old woman. I'm just a girl with white hair. I don't have a voice to tell them men like Uncle Moji are always watching us.

I avoid all men and hate all women. These men who are naturally sinners. These men who still don't know that there will come a day when they'll hang for their weaknesses and burn in Hell. These women who don't yet know how every bit of their existence is dangerous enough to start a flame. They are so dumb that they aren't scared of men like Uncle Moji, or the fires of Hell.

I am in middle school by then, and one day our teacher calls me into her office. The theology teacher's office is full of student documents, theology books, the Quran she uses to teach, a few praise cards, exam papers on the desk, and the kebab she's brought from home. There's a big glass on the desk and a tea flask. The window faces the yard, and since the office is on the ground floor, I can see the students playing outside. A few older kids stick their faces in the window while making funny expressions at me.

The theology teacher takes off her veil and scarf. It's strange to see her suddenly take them off, since I'm used to seeing her with a hijab. "Look," she says, "nobody's watching. No men here. You can take off your veil and scarf."

"Never."

"Do you hear what I'm saying?" She steps toward me.

"You have no right to come near me!" I shout, but she can't hear anything.

She comes closer and closer. "You can take them off. There are no strange men here."

I just look at her.

"Your hair has not been in fresh air for so long, you might pass on a disease to other kids. Do you hear me? The kids have gotten lice, and it's all because of you."

"You're wrong! I don't have lice! They've gotten it from Nazanin. I don't have lice because I never take my scarf off and it protects me from getting them." I scream in my head. This is not fair. Kids aren't strong enough to take direct revenge, so they might as well take revenge indirectly.

She obviously doesn't hear my scream. She touches my veil and scarf, and I scratch her arms so hard, it's as if a cat has scratched her. I bite her arm like a cat whose children are being attacked. She yells out in pain. All the other teachers and the principal rush in.

I stand there, sure they are all going to attack me. But I suddenly have a blackout, and then I don't remember anything. It is all dark. When I open my eyes all the teachers are around me. Maman has come to school and looks at me surprised. I think to myself that they probably have taken my scarf off and have seen my white hair. I touch my head. Everything's in place.

"Sara, you were talking during the blackout. You can talk." The principal comes forward and says, "Sara, darling, get up and look what you've done."

I get up and sit on a chair with the help of some teachers. They bring me water and sugar, chocolate and dates. The janitor even goes to get me bread and cheese.

Our principal shows me a video from her cellphone. I am lying unconscious, talking. What am I saying? I don't know. Neither the teachers, nor Maman who had arrived at the school an hour later, understands what I was saying. I had closed my eyes and said a lot of nonsense, but I was speaking after all.

The theology teacher, who is still rubbing her arm, looks at me with hatred and resentment. I am also surprised to see myself talking nonsense while unconscious. This is my first time speaking since I was seven. It was like my vocal cords showed their natural ability and could stand up among all the bitterness and repression inside me.

"Sara, darling, you can do it! We have to train your ability," says the principal.

Maman sheds tears of joy. My teacher pinches me and calls me a cheeky, wild girl.

2

THE PRINCIPAL CALLS for somebody to see my video, someone who speaks multiple languages. All the teachers, including the theology teacher, wear their hijabs because there is a man coming in. None of the girls at school has ever seen a man in the schoolyard. That's why they are curious to watch him at every possible chance. They all wonder why the mute girl was off school for a couple of days and was drinking tea in the principal's office, and why a man is coming into the school for her.

On this day, I sit on a chair in the principal's office, with tea and cookies in front of me. I can't hide how bad I feel about him coming here to invade our womanly sanctum. Earlier I heard our theology teacher, mumble, "They could probably have found a woman who spoke multiple languages. We didn't need to bring a man in to disturb the school." I have the same opinion but not the voice to express myself or to kick that man out.

The principal shows him the video.

After he watches a bit of it, he pauses the video and comes up to me. It is the first time since the age of seven that a man has come up to me. My hands are sweaty and my body tight. I have to pee, but I tell myself that I have grown up and am not going to do that! The man is holding the phone. As he gets closer to me, I get closer to the barrel of pickles. My cheeks are cold. My body is stiff, like a stick. I feel frozen. With his every movement, I feel worse, and my inner shout climbs closer to my throat. I want to push him away, scratch and bite him so that he'll leave. But I can't. My voice is stuck.

I start to feel like my voice has become a huge gland under my throat.

"Don't go near her because when she was little…" starts the principal.

"No, I have an important question," he says. "Darling, where did you learn that language?"

He keeps inching closer. Every one of my body's cells feels him getting closer. The gland starts melting under my scarf. It escapes my scarf in the form of hair. I am growing hair that covers my chin and my head. As close as he is, he sees hair slipping out from my scarf.

"What is this beard-like hair?" says the man. "What is this excessive hair?"

No one knows.

He approaches me. He reaches out to touch me.

"Don't touch her! Don't you see she's unwell?" the principal yells.

He reaches out. I can feel his heat, and the gland in my throat fizzing silently. Only the women in me hear the fissure. Each voice disappears as it turns into hair and grows out. Many people don't pay attention to how pickle jars explode. When they open the jars, they don't see the bubbles on the surface. They talk too much and don't listen enough. His hands are a millimetre from my head when he jumps back. "What's that smell?"

My stiff body starts shaking. I don't remember a thing from that moment on, only that my chin feels wet. I also pee myself.

3

APPARENTLY, THE MAN told the principal and the theology teachers that the words I uttered were in Polish, and that they were spoken beautifully. To avoid repeating what I felt that day and having another man come to school, they're bringing in a Polish psychologist, who is a first-generation immigrant in Iran, to meet with Maman and me. When she comes in and watches the video, she is surprised and has to listen to it again. Then she calls her aunts in Poland to confirm. After the call, she looks at me.

"Have you ever had a Polish babysitter?" she says.

I remain silent.

"A what?" Maman says.

"A babysitter, like they say in Persian…" She opened her dictionary to 'nanny'.

Maman looks at her miserably. "Wow, how could I ever have afforded that?"

"How about a Polish neighbour, especially an old lady, during her childhood?"

"You should come to see our neighbourhood. There are certainly no foreigners living there. They wouldn't dare come over there even to look."

"Wow." The Polish psychologist comes up to me, pulls at my scarf around my chin. "The hair started growing when that man was here, when he got close to you?"

"Yes. Her chin got wet and smelled acidic," says the principal.

The woman looks at all of us and then at the children behind the door. It's the kind of look you give to people who have hallucinations. "Could you ask the others to leave us," she says to the principal. "Except for me, you, and her." Once everyone leaves, she continues. "Were you scared of the man when he got close to you?"

I nod yes.

She asks our principal to bring in some males for an experiment.

The janitor's husband and her ten-year-old son, both of whom live nearby, are our test subjects. They come in and get close to me, and when they get really close, the gland on my chin explodes with hair, and the acidic smell comes out. The woman looks at me with surprise, and then covers her nose.

"Okay, step back."

As the janitor's husband and her ten-year-old son step a little farther back, the smell goes away.

"The smell is a defence mechanism," the Polish psychologist announces. "It repulses men." She asks the janitor's husband and son to leave again. "I'll tell you something, but do not tell anyone else, and you don't bring her to anybody else because they won't understand. Even I don't understand it. Neither does she. All I can say is that it's an instinct, a defensive instinct with roots in her past. The instinct of becoming a man to confront men! We need to give her time."

She rewatches the video and translates every word I said. Words that, according to the psychologist, only an older, native Polish speaker could utter so perfectly. The words used are archaic words that even the psychologist and her old aunts don't know.

"Here, I'll try to translate for you," she says. "*I started studying at the conservatory two years ago when I was five, but didn't finish. The Russians from the East, the Germans from the West, they invaded our country. They took us on a train to labour camps in Siberia. After a while, my mother and I were sent to Iran via ship. We had never heard of Iran. The others on the ship called it the Fars corridor. We heard Iran was occupied by the Russians from the North and the English from the South. They told us that where we were going, people starved to death because of the attacks from the Russians and the British.*

"They dropped us off at Port Pahlavi. They told us the locals wouldn't let us live there. When we got on the train, Iranians started throwing objects at the train. We said to ourselves: misery again! Hatred again! But they were actually throwing packages of food, since they had heard that we were hungry and that the Russians had taken everything from us. It was the first act of kindness we had received in all our years away from home.

"At Port Pahlavi we lived in the Yusef Abad camp, and one day my mother came in with two other Polish refugees with a plan to escape. They said we had to flee to the city, mix with Iranians so that the Russians and the British wouldn't find us. We fled the camp and slept on the streets for a few nights, until the wife of a wealthy businessman took us in and we officially started working there.

"I learned Persian and became friends with their daughter. We were both teens when, one day, we saw the woman of the house running home with mud on her head, screaming, crying, and hitting herself. She went into the basement and stayed there in punishment for a sin she had committed. A few years later, she died in that basement. She had been out with a veil on, but the extremists during Reza Shah's rule had seen her and stepped on the tail of her veil. The veil tore, and they pulled it off her. She cried and rubbed mud from the riverbank on her head, so nobody would see her hair. She had worn a hijab in front of men her whole life, so for her it was like stripping her naked and assaulting her *in public. That's how ashamed she felt. She grieved until she died, and for the whole time, thought that she would be going to Hell for the sin she had committed, which was appearing in front of strange men without a hijab. But we all knew how kind she was, and if she didn't go to heaven, nobody else would.*

"After that, the Russians and the English began to look for Germans in Tehran. They eventually found us, and from the colour of our skin and our eyes, they gleaned we were Polish and, as they had promised the Iranian government, they sent us to India after the war. India was a British colony, and England had colonized India many years before. I married an Indian man. What can I say about marriage in India..."

And then I was conscious.

"What a sad story. How does she know it?" the principal asks.

The psychologist says that when I talk about the woman's veil, I do so with much propriety and that in the video I hold my scarf tight so that I won't get humiliated, like the woman who died in the basement. The psychologist stares at me. "Do you remember anything from that story?"

My one-hundred-and-fourteen-year-old soul seems to have saved a memory. But my tiny body doesn't know anything about it. I shake my head. No.

The psychologist comes closer and looks at the manly beard on my chin and tries to remove my scarf to see my hair. I raise my hand to scratch her but she winks at me and brings her finger to her nose, shushing me. I calm down. It is the first time someone has removed my scarf to see my white hair. I am scared that she might act surprised, but it's like she already knows what she's about to see. She winks again and pulls my scarf back on.

"I don't think there's a problem with Sara. This Polish-speaking could be a coincidence or a sudden connection to a collective subconscious. Regarding the beard and the smell, I must say, it's a defensive reaction, that's it. Let her be, and don't bother her."

When I leave school that day, a beggar—a kid, a very young one—gives me a piece of paper with a phone number on it, and says, "That lady over there asked me to give this to you."

The Polish psychologist stands across the street, waving at me.

How am I ever going to call her without a voice?

4

THE UNIVERSE, undoubtedly, is an image of what we create collectively, with the power of belief. Maybe, when someone dies, there has been a collective decision made regarding the disappearance of their physical image on Earth. Maybe it is because of collective imaginations that I've been in such misery and haven't been able to speak, only make a few sounds and signs, despite my teachers' hard work. Maybe in order to speak again, I need to change a collective belief about myself. Maybe! Or maybe I am better off alone. Everything has an opposite. For the lonely person nobody is willing to hold, God has arms. I choose for God to become my everything, so that the world I live in is never without an embrace.

The mosque is more helpful to me than school; whenever I hear the Quran, I can repeat it to myself in peace and solitude. It's a bit difficult, but I can stutter some of its words out loud. But other than that, the little girl in me always accepts what the old woman says. The old woman has told me to stay silent forever. "Silence is the best revenge you could take on the world, for yourself and for Setayesh. Silence means Setayesh will live in you forever. Stay silent." Should I? I am torn into pieces, and sometimes I can't tell who is in control, me or the old woman. The old woman knows about revenge, and she knows about years of silence—what it means to absorb everyone like a vacuum. It means knowing when and how to take revenge, to hurt them most.

One day I will explode. Just like the hairy gland that grows under my skin every time I feel threatened, which repulses everyone with its acidic smell and the hair on my chin. This explosion is going to happen one day. I just don't know when or how. Ever since the day I saw death right before my eyes, I was no longer ashamed of violence. Ever since the day I heard Uncle Moji scream, saw his body shake and the pee stain his pants, glands of hatred have been planted in my throat, their roots as strong as the poplar and plane trees of Valiasr Street.

I hate Uncle Moji for assaulting Setayesh. I hate him for cutting my sister into pieces and putting her in the barrel of pickles, in absolute darkness.

I hate Loqman for pushing the swing so lustfully. I

hate him for not defending her and for being silent all these years. I hate him for being a coward.

I hate Baba for running away from his problems and finding peace in something destructive.

I hate Maman for being weak and unable to defend us.

I hate all the people in Tehran for watching the execution with awe and enthusiasm.

I hate everything. The summer, the neighbourhood, the neighbours, the drinking fountain…everyone and everything, even the things I love.

I hate the muezzin whose voice I have fallen in love with. I hate the playful child and the silent old woman in me.

One night, I dream of the kind Polish psychologist who probably knows my secret. In my dream, I am sleeping in a veil and scarf. She wakes me up and I smile at her. She tells me, in Polish, that she has a present for me. I hate her as much as I like her. She smiles at me kindly, just like an angel. She says, "I have a present for you that can put an end to your sorrow, so that you can take revenge on the world."

I can speak perfectly in my dream. I ask her what the present is. She pulls out a machine gun and a knife from under my bed, hands them to me, and says, "Something you can use to take revenge, under one condition. You have to take revenge on anyone who has indulged even the smallest vice."

I hold the machine gun. It's still warm. I jump up and down and say, "All the sadness and the anger are over!" I feel the cold of the knife on my cheeks. The pleasure of the cold feels like revenge. I want to thank her but she's gone. I take the machine gun and suddenly I'm at school, sitting behind a desk, where the girls had bullied me, and the ones who hadn't thought I was slow.

Raana! BANG.

Neda! BANG.

Shima! BANG.

Maryam! BANG.

Their blood splashing on their white scarves and notebooks gives me joy. Now that I think about it, Pani didn't lend me her eraser one day, and Layla always bragged about her pencil case, and it made me jealous. I don't care for Farnaz either, or her straight long hair. Azadeh is too withdrawn, and Maral never studies. Parisa is too studious, and Ayda is fat. In a second, they are all on the ground, covered in blood. I also get a spot of blood on my scarf. I cut that spot out with the knife and put it in Layla's pencil case, which she always bragged about.

The teachers scream and run away. Now that I think of it, our science teacher has yellow teeth, and the social studies teacher is tall. Our theology teacher once called me crazy! And the principal tries too hard to be nice. The janitor has a high-pitched voice. Blood splashes on the walls as I go further.

Outside of school, Loqman and his friends are playing football. They're all shocked when they see me with a machine gun. Loqman bows his head. Plop plop, the sound of the ball bouncing in the blood. I enjoy the beautiful scene.

Uncle Moji is standing a bit farther off. As people run around screaming, he comes over and surrenders himself to me. He knows he's the reason for all of this. He knows I hate him more than anybody in this world. He knows the weapon in my hand is there because of him, and that the other people are all victims of my anger against him. I point the gun at him. I imagine him holding me as a nine-year-old like Setayesh, crushing my bones with his fingers. He hits me until I'm quiet. His saliva falls on my face. The smell of his sweat leaves me breathless. I scream louder. "Sara, help!" And she screams back, "Shut up, Setayesh!" I struggle but he holds me tighter.

He pushes my skirt aside and tears my white underpants away. He says, "You shut up or I'll make you!"

I'm scared, that's why I push and shove vigorously, crying more and screaming louder. "I want my sister Sara. I want Maman and Baba." My body is drenched in his sweat. I don't want this! I don't want to be here alone! Not with this hairy giant who calls me filthy and wants to wash me off with acid. He stinks so bad I can't breathe. I scream, "Sara! Sara, please help!"

He presses his hand over my nose. One two three

four five six seven… his greedy eyes keep getting blurry. And then eternal darkness.

In my dream, I return to Uncle Moji standing in front of me, depressed, putting his hands up. It's like he knows his time has come. People pass us by, running away, screaming. I walk toward him, bring out my cold knife, and shove it in his stomach. His blood pours out. I twist the knife a few times. Maybe this is the most painful death. I keep twisting the knife to let out all the hatred and anger. I empty his stomach and hit his head with the handle of my machine gun until his skull caves in. His greedy eyes become blurry and then give way to eternal darkness.

The reason for my lifelong disturbance dies slowly right in front of me. People are shocked. They are the same ones who watched Uncle Moji's execution when I was a child. What are they doing in my dream?

The people are now watching Uncle Moji's brutal murder. I should probably feel relieved and go back home, but I have also held a grudge against these people. I recall what the Polish woman said: "Even the smallest bad thing!" I point the machine gun at them. In ten seconds all the people in the city are lying on the ground.

On the way home, I see Maman crying. "Sara, what have you done?" Enough crying. Enough being weak. That day, instead of kicking out Baba's useless friends, you sent Setayesh and me out to play.

Pop…

As I get home, Baba wakes up from his nap. "Darling, where were you? Your Maman was so worried! We have already lost a daughter. We can't lose another one." He falls asleep again. I have always been so sick of his irresponsibility. It was his fault that day…

Pop…

The Polish psychologist, that kind angel, is waiting for me beside my bed. "What happened? Did you have fun?"

"Yes, I did. I feel relieved. Everybody got what they deserved."

She smiles, and I can see her teeth. I remember that she was the one who gave me this damn gun to take my revenge. She is the reason for all this sin. I pull out the gun and finish the job as her smile fades. Done.

In my dream, I feel the sweetness of victory and revenge. I can now step on their dead bodies with my boots. I can walk and spit on them. Crush them with my feet, just as they crushed me and my feelings. I cross the street. I walk past the stores, parks, candy and ice cream shops. I have killed everyone. Now I can eat as much ice cream as I want. I can eat jam straight from the jar with my finger, and nobody will say anything. I can eat all the expensive food with nobody to tell me I can't afford it.

Now that nobody's here, I can take off my scarf and let my white hair get some fresh air after a few years. I can wear high heels and walk on the street and act like a grownup.

I can speak loudly, without stuttering. "This is Heaven! Endless happiness!" But even if I speak perfectly, who am I going to talk to?

I shake Raana. "Raana, get up and see my expensive clothes!"

"Maman, get up and see how I can talk now!"

"Baba, get up and see all the money I got from the bank! We can spend it all, and you can buy me all the candy you want!"

"Hey! People! Get up to play, let's go to the park, or even fight. Get up and make fun of my stutter or my face, and hate me, just please get up! Don't lie on the ground indifferently like this!"

Nobody listens to me. They're all dead. I killed them joyfully to be free of even the smallest thing that bothered me. I go to the Polish woman. "Wake up, sweet angel. Can everything go back to the way it was? I want to give the machine gun back. Listen to me, please! I know you can hear me, right?"

Maman wakes me up.

"Sara, darling, why are you crying in your sleep? Your face is all wet."

She is right. My face is all wet. My scarf has wounded my ears. As I cry, I hug Maman very tightly.

"What is this, you're suddenly hugging me?" Maman asks.

I hold her as tight as I can.

"Leave me alone, I have a lot of work to do."

I look at the clock. I'm late for both school and my morning prayer. After the nightmare, which was sweet at the beginning but became very lonely and disturbing toward the end, I now feel a bit lighter. I am slowly beginning to understand that being in my shell is how the world wants to defeat me. Holding a grudge feels like prison. Hatred is poisonous and kills you slowly.

5

THE NEXT DAY AT SCHOOL, while the teacher is calling names, she skips my name as usual and checks my presence. I raise my hand. The whole class turns to look at me.

It is so hard, having all eyes on you. People see you shrink, and all these years I have been silent to be invisible, to be unimportant, and to not feel the heavy weight of their eyes. Being seen and not being seen is like being cheeky and shy, or being selfish and selfless. They're all two sides of the same coin. By wanting to not be seen, I am seen and talked about even more. I am still judged. I die every day to escape death. I exist for others, despite my silence.

I raise my hand. I exist.

The teacher looks at me. "I checked you present, so you don't have to speak. I understand."

I raise my hand again. The whole class turns to look at me again. If I utter the same sounds as before, they will laugh at me. But they are silent and shocked.

"Mmmmmm aaaammmm bbbb ooooo nnnnnn…."

Nobody understands what I'm saying; they all just stare. The teacher doesn't know how to react.

"Do you want to write it down?" she asks.

I shake my head, "No."

I spend so much energy uttering those meaningless sounds that my veil and scarf are soaked in sweat. I repeat them. Nobody understands. All of the muscles in my face, which have become pretty lazy over the years, make unexpected movements to push those sounds out of my throat. My face is shaking, just like someone weightlifting for the very first time.

The other kids start sweating too. I try my best to talk, or at least show the teacher that, from now on, she would have to call my name too.

"Okay, whatever you say!" says the teacher.

I ask her to call on me for the oral examination. She is surprised, but agrees to ask me to read my essay after the break. An essay about what I want to do in the future. Everyone has ten minutes to read their paper, and this is going to be my first time reading mine.

"What are you doing?" says the old woman in me. "You can't do this!"

I yell at her to leave me alone.

"What is this? Why are you rebelling?"

During the break, unlike normally, I don't stay in class. I had seen the last stage of revenge the prior night. I had experienced absolute loneliness in my dream. I get up and go to the schoolyard, where Raana, Neda, and Maryam are playing handball. I join them, jumping up and down, which means *give me the ball*. Raana throws the ball to Maryam. Maryam throws it to Shiva. Shiva throws it above my head to Nahid. Nahid throws it to Maryam, all while I am jumping around to get the ball and join their game. Maryam throws it to Shiva, Shiva throws it to someone else, and so on and so on, to anyone except me!

The ball goes from one person to another until it comes to my hand, either on purpose or unintentionally or out of pity. The ball is in my hand and I am a part of the game.

"Hey, Sara, give it to me!"

"No, throw it to me."

I throw the ball to one of the kids, and for the first time in years I forget that a grumpy old woman with white hair has found a home in me. The child in me starts to play with the same kids she had killed off ruthlessly in last night's dream. But today, they have been given a chance to live. They are running around happily with the wind blowing in their hair, and scarves with no blood stains, all white.

The teacher gives me ten minutes to read my essay. I can hear the kids' chatter and laughter. Even worse, the kids sitting in front of the class impersonate me and make fun of me whenever the teacher looks away. The subject of the essay is "what do you want to be when you grow up?" Those ten minutes feel like ten hours. During the ten minutes, I can only read the first line out loud.

"In the name of God, in the future, I want to become a religious recital lady, read religious stories for women and guide them to the right path."

Two whole pages remain and my time is already up.

"Recital lady?" the kids laugh, "Excuse me, Miss. If Sara becomes a recital lady, it will take her a whole year to recite each story."

"Excuse me, Miss. Nobody will come to her recital, because her face becomes likes this!" they say while impersonating my expressions.

But I know I'm going to be a recital lady. I have memorized all the Surahs and know how to give good advice. I know Hadiths, and for every woman in the mosque who has a question, I have the appropriate answer.

The class has become chaotic and the teacher can't manage. Suddenly we hear applause. The class goes quiet. It's the Polish psychologist. The angel who gave me a machine gun last night in my dream, and whom I killed off. She was standing beside the window, listening to me. Apparently, the teacher had called her during the break, and told her to come to the school when I voluntarily decided to read my paper.

"Good job, Sara! Now promise everyone here that after the New Year holidays you'll perform your first recital here in school, without stumbling."

I don't reply. It's like the old woman, who was gone and had no more control, has come back. Everybody looks at me to see if I will promise or not. I look at her silently and soullessly. One two three four… one hundred… I am silent for a hundred seconds. Everybody else is silent too.

She moves toward me, and whispers, "Will you promise me or should I show your white hair to everyone, old lady?"

The old woman in me steps back, scared. She fears for her reputation. "I pppp…rromise."

The kids, the ones who made fun of me, applaud and say, "Hooray!"

"Write the first line of your recital on this paper! Hang it here on the wall so that everyone will remember what you are going to recite after the holidays, loud and clear."

I write, "I seek refuge with God from the Devil." Everybody writes the same sentence and puts it on the wall for me to remember.

The Polish woman waits for me outside of class. As I go out, she says, "Come over here, I need to talk to you." She takes me to the corner. "Why did you choose that sentence?"

I shrug.

"Is that how you're going to begin your recital?"

"Uhum."

"Why?"

I demonstrate to her that I am more comfortable writing. She lets me write to her.

She takes a few steps back. "Do you think the Devil is a man or a woman?"

"Mmmaaan."

"A man, how interesting. What about God?"

"Mmmaaan." I explain that, in Arabic, God is spoken of with male pronouns.

"That's interesting. But what about women?"

I don't understand what she means.

"I'm coming to your school after the holidays." She looks at me and leaves.

I am a woman who wants to be God's best creature, the God I choose to believe in, the world's mother who embraces us even in times when we have nobody.

6

During the holidays, I stand in front of the mirror and say out loud, "I seek refuge with God from the Devil." My facial muscles tighten up, my tongue becomes numb, my body overheats. I sweat. But I keep saying it. I can say it in my mind perfectly, many times. But as soon as I make a sound, it becomes a stutter. At night, when everyone is asleep, I put my mouth on the pillow and say, "I seek refuge with God from the Devil." I mumble it everywhere, like a witch putting out a spell. I mumble it without a struggle.

Then the holidays are over. It's the first day back at school. My hands are frozen and I know the Polish psychologist will show up any moment.

"Have you prepared your speech?" the kids ask sarcastically.

I am overwhelmed with fear. But I know if I get scared this time, if I become the victim, if I don't try to plan my whole life, I will become silent and useless again, and my whole life will be filled with anger toward Uncle Moji and tormented thoughts of Setayesh, and the old woman telling me every day how I've destroyed myself. I just need to be free and let go of the past, to feel for once like there's a future.

I stand in front of the class. Raana rolls her eyes and Maryam makes impressions. I close my eyes and imagine myself above all of them, in the mosque, on the stage, speaking for women. Raana and Maryam, along with everyone else, are sitting in the front row, wearing veils, listening intently.

"Open your eyes!" the Polish psychologist says.

I take a breath and say, "Aaaaaaaaaaa……."

Everybody laughs. I am sweating. My veil sticks to me. I see the Polish psychologist's worried eyes. She doesn't want me to fail! *She* doesn't want to fail! I remember how she threatened to show my hair to everyone.

"Aaaaaaaaa…"

They laugh again.

"Everybody, quiet!" the Polish psychologist says.

When I imagined this moment, I could speak without stuttering. But now I can't. I feel dizzy for a second, and see Setayesh standing in the dark, looking at me. It's so bright behind her that I can't see her innocent face. It's like she's waiting for me to push ahead. It's as if she's begging, "Please leave me and that disastrous day alone. Your pain is hurting me!"

I overcome myself. I see myself as a recital woman, reading a sermon. One woman asks me: My husband hits me, what should I do? Another woman asks: Is the prayer for the dead obligatory or optional? Should I say it for my mother-in-law? Will a nine-year-old girl go to Hell for not wearing a hijab? I imagine myself communicating easily. They all look at me with envy, envy of my knowledge and my speaking abilities. I talk about God, the Prophet Muhammad, and how religion is our only saviour. About how women who don't wear the hijab will not go to heaven. About how we should pray five times a day, and how much God loves us. About how there is Heaven and Hell, and we all achieve justice in the end, and how we will go to Hell if we seduce a strange man.

In the mosque, everybody looks at me with admiration and envy, and they wish they knew as much about the afterlife. They envy not having been as innocent as I was. They have shown their hair to men and been touched by them. My sermon ends with the school bell. I say, "To wrap it up, please say Salavat!"

They become silent for a moment. Absolute silence. They are shocked, but then after a second, they say Salavat and applaud. Raana stands up in front of me. So do the rest of the kids. I see myself in the classroom. The Polish psychologist is crying, and so is our teacher.

They hug me. Everybody hugs me.

"Ohhh the bbbeeeellll ranngggg sooo soon!" I say.

"Good job Sara," the Polish psychologist says. "You were reciting the whole time!"

I stutter again, but the Polish psychologist says it's normal and that I will keep getting better. "You spoke nonstop for us."

I don't remember anything from my recital. But I think we all come to this planet for a reason.

7

SOME DAYS I SEE MAMAN talking to Setayesh's photos. I now see how the world is a strange place. We're left here to get as much attention as we want, for some to become stronger and others to become weaker. To start thousands of games to gain attention. To hit and be hit. And then there's death. In death, everything is neutral. Not meaningless, but without preference. In death, there is no hitting or being hit, no questions and no answers. It's like there's a wall between the two worlds: one cries and can't hear the other one speaking. Maman talks to Setayesh for hours. Setayesh also lives in my eternity, but in her world, she is silent. Death is the realest form of loneliness.

As I say these things, I realize I have also been dead for years. I don't hit or get hit. I don't love or let myself be loved. I was stuck at being seven, and that's why the one-hundred-and-fourteen-year-old woman invaded me. I killed myself off at seven, and religion came to my aid, became my safe place; but it isn't my cure, it's a preservative just like the one they use for pickles.

Ever since that day in school, the whole neighbourhood calls me in whenever they can afford a recital woman. I have come out of my shell, and religion is now my way to reconnect with people. People come to me and I advise them that if their children don't study, they must read the Surah an-Nur chapter of the Quran to resolve the problem. Sometimes I give them water from the Zamzam fountain to make them feel better. And people are happy that I exist. They are glad they have someone they can talk to. The prayers calm them down and this is the cure I offer them.

I am glad to be alive and to be able to help and listen. I still stutter sometimes, but during recitals I speak perfectly. The old woman is getting used to me and complains less, even as she comes with me wherever I go, except when I step on a scale. Only I know the burden of carrying this person.

In our neighbourhood, even older women correct their hijabs whenever they see me. If I see a nine-year-old girl, I touch her hair and say, "Darling, wear a hijab. Take care of yourself, and let your beauty be seen by those close to you, and only show your ugliness to the world so you'll always be safe." And every time I say that I cry a bit. If I see their mothers, I force them to cover their daughters. The mothers scream at me, and I insist more.

Now everything is different. I have become a favourite student. The other kids obey me, and Raana, Maryam and Nazanin have become my group of friends. After school, I order them to stalk girls who have secret meetings with their boyfriends. As soon as we catch them, I chase the girls with scissors and cut their hair, and threaten the boys to make them run away. The principal and counselor's jobs have become much easier. They have someone who takes their jobs more seriously, and they still get a salary from the government. My group finds all the girls who pluck their eyebrows or remove facial hair. I warn them once, and if they don't listen to me, I report them to the principal, who lowers their grades.

I now have the power to control them all. I was the silent Sara, the suffering Sara. The tables have turned and now they are the ones who suffer. The only thing that hasn't changed is my veil and scarf. With my young age and my stutter, I am now the rich, religious women's favourite girl in town. Every weekend, they fight over who gets to have me at their house, and they pay me well for their private audience.

Every Thursday night I start with cursing the Devil and saying hello to God and his Prophet. If the session is a celebration, I speak positively, and if the session is to mourn, I say the same things in a more painful way.

People cry either way. They like it when someone like me speaks for them, so that they can dig deep within themselves and cry. They calm down by crying. They are scared of feeling happy and that's why they pay me to make them cry. The more painfully I describe an event, the more they cry. I always finish with a sentence that leaves them feeling better about their plight.

My talent for speech has become my power. In the pulpit, I am a step above everyone else. I like this job because each time they turn off the lights, I can weep for Imam Hussein, for Setayesh, for the old woman, for myself, and for all victims of oppression. This is how I pay my dues to Setayesh, to fight back against freedom and joy in this oppressive world where happiness is a sin. This is the philosophy of me.

PART THREE

Fighting

1

In high school, I decide to study theology. I want to study theology and go to the women's school of theology. Our high school principal is sure I will get into college, so she arranges a meeting to introduce me to one of the college's best professors. As the principal is writing the name and number on a piece of paper, she asks, "The professor is a man. Is that okay with you?"

My throat suddenly feels frozen. I can feel little balls of hair moving under my skin, wanting to get out like a beard. They put a lot of pressure on my chin, and I fear the glands could explode at any moment and wet my neck with acid. I remain silent and leave the office, slamming the door behind me. I go to the backyard and start crying for the first time in years. Just like that, Setayesh is in me, screaming and moving again in the dark place with the acidic smell where she's locked up.

I curse theology school, and how unfair it is to need a male teacher there. Why should I go through all this?

The principal finds me crying. "Take this tissue. I just spoke to the professor, and he agreed to speak to you over the phone."

It's my first time talking to a man. I have to do it. I'm aiming for Heaven so I need to pass through this Haji. I call him. Maman and Baba aren't supposed to find out. If they do, they will be very excited that I am finally speaking to a man, and I'm not in the mood for their excitement.

"Hello?" I hear the Haji's deep voice. "Hi Miss. I have been waiting for your call. Your principal told me about you. You don't have to speak if you're uncomfortable. I'm going to introduce myself first, and then explain my teaching approach. Then you can make up your mind, and if you're ready, we'll start lessons next week."

His voice is warm and soothing, like a prophet preaching theism and peace. He's nothing like the vile image I have of men based on my Baba and his friends, Uncle Moji, and Loqman. He has a beautiful voice, just like the muezzin, maybe even better. He comes from another planet, or maybe from heaven.

"Should we start next week?" he asks.

Next week? It's too late. I don't say anything.

"Okay, so if you agree, I'll wait for you to call me next Tuesday, around the same time. And if you don't call, I'll take it to mean disagreement."

And then he hangs up.

A week from now is too late. It means seven nights. Why didn't I say anything? Why have I gone back to my mute ways?

Days go by, and all I think about is next Tuesday. In school, my group of girls reports that one of the students has tweezers. I am searching her backpack when I suddenly see the principal talking to a theologian. I find the tweezers. All the girls gather around and the theologian looks at me. I lose the tweezers. I pull my veil tighter and let go of the backpack.

"What do we do? Did she have tweezers?" the girls scream.

"No, she didn't. Leave her alone," I say.

The girls' arguing grows louder, and I hide behind a pillar to avoid eye contact with him. I see him, but not clearly. Is that the Haji whose voice has taken my heart? What is he doing here? What if he's in love with me too? Do I want to get married? What kind of man is he? Would I be happy? I feel butterflies in my stomach. It isn't that I'm worried; it's a different kind of sensation I have never felt before. Is he the father of my future children?

I hear the girl whose backpack I'm still holding. "Are you ashamed of yourself now? Is it your business to check my stuff? In other countries, this would be considered an invasion of privacy!"

Raana yells at her and says the principal herself had

given me permission to search her bag. "Sara is the principal's representative, and you need to respect her!"

All the other girls start cursing us the way they curse the morality police and the authorities.

After the man leaves, I walk up to the principal.

She looks at me. "What is it?"

I don't say anything.

"That was your professor. He was afraid you were scared of him over the phone. Do you want to take lessons from him?"

I leave without replying.

The girl who had the tweezers comes up to me. "You should apologize! In front of everyone!"

I push her aside.

She continues. "You can only use your force on us. When there's a man around, you become so desperate you can't even stand ten kilometres away from him."

Everybody laughs. Even the girls in my group. I look at them. The girls in my group go silent.

"If you don't stop, I'll take your tweezers to the principal," I whisper to her. I stutter it, yet she understands me. She stops talking, and I leave.

When I get home, I head straight to my room, as always. I take off my layers and bring out the mirror from behind my closet. Without the cloth to cover me and hide me from myself, I touch my hips. I can feel all the fat and meat hanging off them. I take off the rest of my clothes, even though it is hard and I am scared.

When did I gain all the weight? My belly pops out on the side view. When did it form? All the fat is here to protect me, but from whom? Myself, or others?

I touch my belly and bum. I touch my wheat-coloured skin, full of spots. My hands are as soft as Setayesh's. As soft as a naughty little girl. I feel Uncle Moji's hands on my hips. He touches my soft skin and then puts his hand on my mouth. I feel a tingling in my throat. The hairy glands want to get out and see the sunlight. I put my pants back on. I have to pee.

I don't need all this fat on my body. There's a man out there that I'm falling in love with. A kind man with whom I don't need the fat for protection.

I pick up the phone and call the kind Haji. He doesn't pick up. I call again. He doesn't pick up. What if he was offended by my rudeness and regretted the offer to be my teacher? The old woman starts laughing and says, "Take your scarf off in front of the mirror, if you dare!" I look at myself, standing in front of the mirror, wearing a scarf and underwear. I pull the scarf back and the messy white hair springs out. I frown.

The old woman laughs. "Do you really think this man is single? He has kids and a wife. Wives, even! I know these kinds of men."

A monster is coming out. I move the mirror back behind the closet. That image of me almost naked is gone, but I can still see my reflection behind the closet. I turn off the light, remove the scarf and hide under the blanket.

The phone rings a couple of times, but I don't dare move.

I am in love with this Haji but there's a problem. I love this man, and I see my future with him, even though he surely has a wife. I don't care about this woman. I know these kinds of men don't have a good relationship with their wives. He is safe. He is kind and he won't abuse me. He will be happier with me. He has to be mine.

What I'm doing is neither moral nor logical. No! This world owes me. Anything secret or wrong helps me feel equal to the world. Everyone has their own way of fighting. One becomes a wolf, and another becomes a fox.

The good news is that I have discovered the secret of the universe. In that sense, I don't care if Haji will be mine or not. I know that when I dream, I die regardless of my mistakes and immaturity. A window opens for me in my darkest time. I dream that life is beautiful, even in its last breath.

2

I AM SUPPOSED TO MEET him by the school. I plan to use my feminine instincts to attract this man, who is the first one I've ever loved.

A cool breeze blows. I see him approach the school's back door. He walks toward the school as his driver waits at the other end of the street. Love makes the street smell like new asphalt, but in fact the asphalt is old and full of holes and bumps. I try to focus and tell myself not to pay attention to the rusty school door or the breeze or the driver, the leaves floating in the wind, the uphill street, or the trees. Only pay attention to Haji, to myself, only the two of us, me and the man I love.

As he steps past the school's fence, my glands start getting bigger, and thick black hair starts sprouting out of my face, just like a growing tree. He gets closer and closer and I pee myself. He sees me, desperate and defenceless.

"Don't be scared. I'm not going to hurt you." He starts praying. "Those who have believed and whose hearts are assured by the remembrance of Allah. Unquestionably, by the remembrance of Allah, hearts are assured."

His voice calms me down. God's memory is soothing to our hearts! But now there is a flood coming out of my eyes. There are fluids coming out of my body, from everywhere! It's as if all the fear I have is leaving my body.

"Get away and leave me," I say with the unknown male voice.

Haji becomes silent.

He pauses for a second. He takes a few steps back. I can see fear in his eyes. He looks at me as if saying, "Is this a trap? Here? On an empty street behind the school's back door?" He waves to his driver. I can see the driver in the background drop his cigarette on the ground, get in the car and drive toward us. He is frightened and time passes so slowly for him.

The man in me is going crazy, not knowing what to defend, and doesn't listen to anyone. I am afraid of myself too. I am afraid of this advocate who doesn't know what to do or what he wants from me.

The driver arrives. Haji gets in the car without looking back. I can smell the smoke from the exhaust as the car drives off. They disappear around the corner.

Nothing more of them can be seen. He has left and I am left behind, with Setayesh, the man, the old woman, and many more unknown creatures.

The school bell rings. Students begin streaming out of classrooms. I have to disappear. Tomorrow I have to get back to busting girls with their boyfriends.

3

I HAVE GIVEN MY HEART. It's like his face is calling me. I have to be his and he has to be mine. This Haji is a well-known man, wanted by many women though he belongs to his wife. But I must do whatever it takes to have him for myself. Only then will justice prevail.

While walking to school, I come across the street where the Polish psychologist's office is. I go in. The secretary asks me if I have an appointment or not. I don't respond and just sit down. The office isn't that big. There are two vases as big as me right next to the secretary's desk, then a drinking fountain, and a few magazines on the table in the waiting room. The secretary yells at me and asks me to leave, and says the doctor is busy and I don't have an appointment. She's lying. There's nobody else in the office. But the Polish psychologist is the only person in the world who would see me whenever I want. To her, I am an interesting case. I cover my ears while the secretary yells.

The secretary approaches me, and I start screaming. The Polish psychologist comes out of her office.

"Sara! How did you get here?"

The secretary looks at me and apologizes, and says that she thought I didn't have an appointment.

"How did you get here?" she repeats. "Are you alone?"

It is my first time going there all by myself. I have come to ask for her help with my problem—to stop shaking and peeing every time a man approaches. Even worse, to help with the beard that grows on my face that no doctor can cure with hormonal treatment.

In the psychologist's office, there is a comfortable couch. The lights are dim, and she keeps a few cactus plants on the table. Her chair is by the window. On the wall she has hung a circular sign.

"This is yin and yang," she says. "Do you know it?"

I don't care about yin, yang, or anything else. I just want to get to the man whose voice I have fallen in love with, and who is behind obstacles such as his wife and how far we must stand from one another. There are many things in my way. I am scared. I write her the whole story, my love story, and I mention at the end that he has to be mine.

She laughs and says, "You see? You are assaulting his wife. Can you see there is a weak woman here, and you are going to break the balance of her life?"

I can't imagine his wife. I am blind. I will never see her. I can just replay what has happened to me. I write down that there are lots of women inside me, and recently I have found a man as well. There is a man emerging in me, and he's the one who spoke and made the theologian run away.

"We're all both man and woman, both good and bad. We are everything. Don't overthink it. You just have to get used to it." She laughs.

I want to ask her: How do I get used to this old woman? The man? Setayesh? And all the dead women who have been reborn inside me? I need to get rid of the one who wants to pick up a machine gun and kill everyone.

"Get rid of yourself, Sara!" she replies, without me asking. "You are invading other people's boundaries without realizing it."

Me? But I don't invade people's lives! They invade mine.

4

THE POLISH PSYCHOLOGIST doesn't charge me, but she doesn't help me either. Just like the life I've known all these years, I only have God. My home is the mosque where I first sought refuge.

I pull aside my veil and lie on the ground in the mosque, and stare at the ceiling's paisley pattern. One orange two oranges three oranges four oranges… In my dream, I see myself in a field. A girl with long hair is holding my hand and running with me. Her hair flashes in the wind. We both run and laugh in the field.

"I like the wind in our hair," I say without a stutter.

"The wind? In your hair?" she laughs.

I touch my head, but there is no hair. She keeps running and laughing.

"Wait! I don't have hair. I'm bald!"

I'm scared. She reaches out and removes my scarf. I scream.

"You have to get rid of yourself," she says. She transforms into the Polish psychologist.

I scream again. The wind in my hair feels disgusting.

She laughs. She asks me if we can ride bicycles together. She pulls at me.

I cry. I say, without stuttering, that I can't ride a bicycle.

"Come with me, don't be scared." She pulls my hand.

I want my scarf back. I feel so heavy it's like I'm stuck to the ground. I hold myself but she keeps pulling me. She is as light as a kite, but I just keep holding myself tight. Gravity is holding me back. I'm as heavy as she is light. That's why we don't move. We just keep pulling each other. We eventually let go. She flies away like a kite, and I fall to the ground and get pulled into the earth, where I hear the Azan—the soothing sound of God.

I open my eyes and see the ceiling full of beautiful flowers. I calm down. What a strange dream it was. Who was that joyful girl? Setayesh in heaven? No, it wasn't her. Was it me? No! Was it the old woman as a young girl? What did she want to do with me?

"Come to pray, come to true prosperity, come to pray." God is inviting me to worship him and do good deeds. I put on a man's turban and a woman's veil, and start to pray. "In the name of God, the gracious and merciful. I pray the evening prayer, for the sake of closeness to God."

A girl passes before me. I know her. But who is she?

"I take refuge with the Lord against the evil of the rejected Devil."

Dear God, I am focused on you and worshipping you. But I've seen this girl somewhere.

"Proclaim, 'He is the one and only God. The absolute God.'"

She knows me too. I've seen her somewhere.

"Our Lord, give us in this world that which is good and in the Hereafter that which is good, and protect us from the punishment of the Fire."

The image of the field returns before my eyes. Two women walking with baby strollers, going to get coffee. I've never seen them, but they look like an image I've seen before. Two women, one wearing shorts, the other a skirt.

That girl is Natasha from Old Montreal! The image I'm seeing is brunch. Why would she show up in my dream? Why does she want to make me get rid of myself? I only spent the one evening with her, when my mother served guests at her mother's party. Why would she join me that day in the field? I finish my prayer. I have to go home. Natasha's image disappears.

I have to see Haji. I have to tell him I'm not a man. I have to tell him to not fear me. It doesn't matter if my voice becomes deep or I grow a beard, I am still the vulnerable woman he has been sent to save. When I wake up in the morning, I think to myself that I won't be able get rid of myself overnight, but that I could do it slowly. I leave a note for Maman that says I have extra classes today and will be home by night.

But I skip school instead. I go to the terminal and, keeping away from men, get on a bus to Qom. I arrive in Qom by noon. I write 'the Seminary' on a piece of paper and give it to the taxi driver, from whom I shrink away as far as I can in the backseat. When I get there, I stand under a tree and look at everyone who comes in and out. Finding him in a large area like this is almost impossible. But I have faith that I will find him on this day.

Faith is always a miracle. He comes out of the seminary. He passes by me like a slow-motion film, and he sees me. My throat heats up. Time stops. We look at each other. He doesn't wait like I do. He walks past me. He's holding hands with a woman wearing a chador. I can only see her eyes. He pulls her along and continues on his way.

That's it!

The whole world goes silent. With everything happening at a slower speed, the details linger too long right before my eyes. In the extended moment, I see the love I have sparked in him. After coming all this way with my nonexistent courage, he passes by me with his wife. Is she beautiful? Is she old? Or sweet? What does she look like?

Everything has paused. Even my glands don't know whether they should explode or go back to sleep. How could he hold hands with a woman? The old woman inside me says, "He is human, just like all the other men. He probably loves his wife!"

"Probably!" I say to myself. My legs feel numb.

That night when I get home, I take Baba's cellphone and text the psychologist about what happened.

She writes back straightaway. "At least you realized how powerful you are! To travel alone and face one of the challenges of this world all by yourself! I am proud of you!" She is right; how can I, being the secretive and fearful person that I am, be so brave? I went to another city, alone, and faced a world of surprises. I have always surprised myself. I am not how others describe me. Who am I? Who should I get rid of?

I want to ask all the women in me who had lived on this planet for many years, if they know the secret of the centipedes and how many feet they have. And I know that if I ever ask, the old lady will laugh and say, "What kind of question is that? Does it even matter? All that matters is that this life is full of oppression and injustice, and we must take revenge!"

I believe her. After I read the Polish psychologist's reply one more time, I delete both messages.

5

I AM STILL AT WAR WITH myself. I am in the women's section of the mosque, lying on the rug on the floor, staring at the ceiling. The flowers are from Heaven, and the dome points to God above me. I hear a man weeping in the men's section. He is seeking help from the Imam of the mosque. He is seeking help from religion, to get answers, as a man who has lost his sons in the Iran-Iraq war and during the Islamic Revolution, about whether his daughter who was recently killed in city demonstrations is a martyr as anti-government groups believe, or an agitator as the government calls her.

I know the answer from the Quran. *O humanity! Indeed, we created you from a male and a female, and made you into peoples and tribes so that you may get to know one another. Surely the most noble of you in the sight of Allah is the most righteous among you. Allah is truly All-knowing, All-aware*, it is written in Surah Hajarat Ayet 13. The sobbing man's daughter is a martyr, I want to shout.

But the Imam of the mosque says he feels sick and has to leave early. The sound of the poor man weeping can be heard from the altar. In times of need, we reach out to God because we ignore the signs around us and expect answers from above.

"Why me? Why me?" he calls out. But nobody has the answer.

He cries so loud that other people can't pray. He cries and says that he no longer has children to sacrifice for his country. He cries and says that dying has become the job of the people of this country. He wants an answer from religion about whether he will go to Heaven or not after sacrificing his three children. He wants to know if the martyrdom of his two sons is enough to compensate for an agitator of a daughter, if she is considered one, and still go to Heaven.

I want to tell him that he can talk to me, but I know that, as a woman, nobody will pay me much attention. Everything is more credible from men, even for some women. But I have the answer. I can use a thousand verses to prove that God has seen his good work. What's important is that he has faith. What's important is that... I can bring up a thousand verses to calm him down, but I don't know if his daughter is a martyr or an agitator. Maybe she was just passing by when she took a bullet to her heart. I don't know if this poor man will go to Heaven or not.

The man can't stop crying. I slide slowly along the rug. I feel responsible for him, like a doctor under oath who runs into an ill person while on a break. I have to make him feel better. I feel a responsibility toward him and anyone else who is devoted to religion and needs answers. I have to give him an answer to calm him down, no matter what.

I feel courage in me. I stand up and head toward the men's section. With every step that I take, the different parts of me become louder, screaming, "What are you doing?" The old woman groans and wants me to stay in the corner of the mosque. But I don't see a point in not helping. The closer I get to the men's section, the stronger my male scent smells and the bigger the throat gland grows. Hairs find their way onto my chin.

I can't enter the men's section. I'm not accepted there. I am nobody to people who are devoted to religion, because women in religion, at their best, can only be followers. So I make a turban out of my hijab and place it on my head. I pull the curtain aside. The male scent gets stronger as hair covers my face and neck. There he is, crying. Everyone else has left, and there is no one else in this part of the mosque, only the man and me.

As I walk toward him, the beard keeps growing longer on my face, until he finally turns back and sees me. How old is he? How old is a man who has lost three children? One hundred? Two hundred? He is a thousand years older than what he should be. Whenever a man or a woman suffers, they become old, by a hundred or a thousand years.

He looks at me and bows. He stops crying. "You are the Prophet Yusuf as you've come to see me," he says. "You are so beautiful." He kisses my hand and returns to the altar to pray.

When he bows down for sujud, I go back to the women's section, put my veil back on, and I can breathe again. The beard slowly disappears. I look at him from behind the curtain. His hand is up while praying, and he smiles. He has gotten his answer, without me saying anything. In me, he has seen someone who gave him an answer. In me, he has seen the answer.

Now I have seen the answer too. Now I know why God has given me a beard, and why there is a man with a deep voice in me. This man is the courage and the voice of all the women in me. I was looking for answers outside myself. I didn't believe in myself. I didn't listen to the galaxies as I searched for something beyond me. Oppression makes us lose our confidence. I have to work for all the women in me and regain all the rights that men have taken from them.

People from all beliefs and religions want a man as their Messenger. This is not a world of men and women, but a world of men who require everything to be as they want it. They are powerful and have strong arms. But now that I have a beard and a manly voice, I want to do something to impact all the oppression we have faced. I am the only woman who can hide behind the man in me and fight back.

6

THE MOSQUE I HAVE CHOSEN has a short wall between the men's and women's bathrooms. The bathrooms smell bad, and there is water on the floor due to people using it for ablution before prayer. Its white mosaics are muddy from people walking in and out.

Putting on my veil, I go to the women's bathroom, quickly change my clothes and put on a turban to cover all my white hair. I climb over the short wall into the men's bathroom and enter the men's section of the mosque. There, the men pray behind me, and ask me their religious questions, and I give them short answers or indirectly assign someone else to answer them, because from what I know, I am still a woman and ashamed to talk about some subjects.

Afterward, back in the women's section, there are women coming in and saying their men have changed, and that is probably the best thing for me to hear. The old woman in me laughs and says these men were born and raised by women. It was their mothers who had raised them like this, to repress and control women. Force women.

I now divide my time equally between both sections. I am a woman and, when I pass the curtains in the centre of the mosque, I am a man. To me, the world of men was always unknown and scary. I didn't like these human beings who wanted to abuse their physical power and manipulate the world. But now the universe gives me this opportunity to know them better. The responsibility of being powerful sits heavy on my shoulders. They carry this title, and they hide their tears behind their loud voices and hide their emotions behind their arms. They don't have the right to be themselves either. They are alone, and they are sometimes victims too. They have needs, deep emotions and fears just like us. I feel sorry for them.

The men also like me, because I am not like the others—I actually listen to them. One day, while the men are praying behind me, Setayesh's voice rises up from the dark place with the acidic smell, crying for help. It has been years since I've heard it. After the prayer, I feel dizzy. I see something familiar from the corner of my eye. I turn to look in its direction. He's there, in the rows of praying men behind me. Loqman. I can hear his voice saying, "Let's play doctor."

Our eyes meet. At first he's silent and scared, but then he smiles and nods out of respect. My throat bloats. It doesn't matter that the beard has already grown; it wants to explode and grow more hair.

"Seyed! Keep me in your prayers!" Loqman says.

It suddenly smells like Baba's guests. Is it Loqman who smells like Baba's guests? It's a heavy smell that resembles disappointment. The smell of being a victim. I feel sick. I want to pee. I want to say it smells like pickles in here. But I just drop my head. I don't know what to say.

Even as I look away, Loqman approaches me. "I have a problem that I need to share," he confesses. "I've been told the Imam of this mosque is the most humane and knowledgeable among them all. Do you have time?"

Humane? Knowledgeable? I don't want to help him. I don't want him there. He should have been executed with Uncle Moji. It was all his fault. It was all because Setayesh liked him. He shamelessly protected Uncle Moji, and later screamed with joy at his execution. But I have sworn to help everyone in the mosque, between God and me, without discrimination, and without hesitation. This mission requires responsibility, and I have accepted that. But I could harm this one so bad. He deserves it. I must give him orders that will torment him and give him a good lesson.

After prayers, the mosque empties and I am alone

with Loqman. His hands are shaking. He says he has a problem and a question. He says, "I know that marriage is the tradition of Muhammad, but I am afraid of it." He says that he has met a girl but he overheats and feels sick every time he sees her. "I have an image in my mind from my childhood that stops me from approaching girls."

I am silent. Setayesh is listening too. He says that he has been indecisively messing with the girl and doesn't know if he wants to marry her or not. I want to say something, or even attack him. I don't feel well. I want to tell him that his is a world of punishment and he should die in his conscience. But I just listen.

He's shaking. I'm shaking. I feel like crying. He says he has thoughts that keep him from sleeping. I want to tell him that he deserves it and has to tolerate the pain he has caused me and my family forever, but he keeps on talking.

"When I was a child there was a man in our neighbourhood that everyone called uncle," he says with a raspy voice. He confesses to me that this man had assaulted him multiple times as a child, and gave drugs to his father in exchange for his son. To keep him from screaming out of pain, he used to put opium on his skin to numb the pain. He said that the man had told him if he said anything about this to anyone, he would turn in his father, who was an addict and a drug dealer, and his father would be executed. After each time he was assaulted, this uncle would beat him because he believed the little boy had stimulated him to sin.

With his hands shaking, Loqman says that he still uses opium. He can't live without opium, although he knows it's not good. He's stressed out. He still can't deal with the past, and doesn't want to admit that he's never loved a woman, even the one in his life right now who has helped him quit opium on and off. He says that he's unable to sleep.

Something is ringing in my brain. Why do I feel like Setayesh is crying and Loqman has embraced his love for her? As Setayesh cries for her childhood love, I listen to the ringing in my mind: that's why Loqman's family didn't say anything to the police! They were also in trouble.

"This is how Loqman was raised to understand love," Setayesh screams from among the pickle barrels. "Forgive him for me, Sis."

I feel dizzy. I close my eyes and calmly say, "Loqman, you are innocent. You're a victim too. Setayesh has forgiven you. Go on and live a peaceful life with the woman who loves you and has stood by you in sobriety."

His eyes open in shock as he hears his name and Setayesh's name. He starts shaking and crying. "Who are you?" He bows to me. "You are a miracle. How did you know my name? Do you see Setayesh in the other world? Is she okay? Is she in Heaven?"

Setayesh is inside me, I want to say. She has become eternal, deep in my soul. I nod yes. I leave him crying on the carpet and disappear to the men's bathroom, where I throw up. With nobody around, the beard starts to recede as I cross back over the short wall to the women's side. Feeling sick, I forget to check if there is anyone in the women's bathroom. A woman sees me and screams, then runs to the women's section. I enter into a bathroom stall and put on my veil.

The woman who saw me in the bathroom comes back into the bathroom with two guards. I hold my veil tight. She smirks as she watches me leave.

As soon as I get home, Maman says, "Your face has changed."

Why, what has happened to my face?

"You look like a child. Are you happy?"

Am I happy? I don't know. All I know is that a heavy weight has been taken off my shoulders. Everything has changed. I am not the Sara I was before.

The phone rings. It's the Polish psychologist. "Sara, what have you done? Come to my office as soon as you can."

I remember how the woman smirked at me, as if to say "I got you!"

7

THE POLISH PSYCHOLOGIST is sitting at her desk when I enter her office. Without even saying a word, she opens Instagram and shows me a video. It's an interview with the woman from the mosque, who says that she saw the Sheikh leaving the mosque wearing a veil. There are other people saying there is no way he could hide the whole beard behind a veil. The woman says that she is almost sure that the beard is artificial and that the Sheikh removed it.

The video also features Loqman saying with enthusiasm that the Sheikh had a strange power and knew about the past and the future. Loqman confirms that the Sheikh he saw was a man, probably a teenager, masculine, but better in his clairvoyance and wisdom than other men. If the Sheikh was a woman, he concludes, then she was a messenger from God with special powers.

"The messenger has the power to switch genders!" shouts a girl standing behind the news reporter. Others in the crowd begin to shout their opinions too. "There will never be another prophet after Mohammed!" "Of course He has the power to be young and live as both genders!" "It's a miracle!"

"Do you understand what you've done?" the Polish psychologist asks. "The whole city is looking for you. What if you get caught?"

But people like me.

"Sara, do you understand? They're going to kill you. Because you're a woman, you fooled the people and, in addition, you didn't have right to pass beyond the curtain in the mosque to enter the men's section."

"What do I do now?"

"Stay here for now. You're not going home."

"I just wanted to help. I just wanted to know men and teach them how to treat women."

She checks the tagged Instagram pages on the video. In just a few hours, dozens of fan pages for The Sheikh of the Mosque have been created, the number of followers increasing every second. "They're calling you a virtual prophetess!"

In another video, the warden at the mosque says, "I also don't know where this Sheikh has come from. We have asked the authorities, and nobody new was assigned here. You may not believe it, but no one has ever seen this person come and go, and there are no records on security cameras. This is a special person. We just have to wait and see if the Sheikh will come back tomorrow."

Special person? Me? Over the next hours, I am surprised by the number of pages talking about what I've told them during my short time in the mosque. The woman who has lived in me for one hundred and fourteen years seems impressed. She says, "Your followers are rising more rapidly than an actual prophet." Some of them are fans of real prophets from the past. Others are part of the miracle of social media, which can make a big bubble out of anything. The extent of the attention is scary and, of course, sweet.

By evening, the Polish psychologist is so scared she keeps looking out her window for signs of trouble. "I can't let you stay here any longer," she says. "You must leave tonight. Even staying here until morning is dangerous. Having this many fans is going to create problems. The people who become your fans blindly can also become your enemies blindly."

"But I have no place to go."

"If you want to stay alive, you should go tonight." Then she adds, "I know just the place."

8

THE ROOM HAS TALL WINDOWS, paintings from the world wars, and a Persian carpet on the floor. It is filled with the sweet smell of rosewater, saffron, cardamom and pistachio. The Polish ambassador eats Persian cookies while watching the video in which I spoke Polish. While I sit across from him, I feel heat welling up in my throat and hair starting to grow on my chin.

"How do you know Polish?" he asks with his heavily accented Persian.

"She doesn't know Polish, but she spoke it once when she was unconscious," says the Polish psychologist.

They start talking in their language. I don't know a word in Polish, yet I understand every word they say. The psychologist says to the ambassador, "We come from a country that was destroyed during the Second World

War, where many innocent people became homeless. My family escaped and was accepted through the hospitality of Iranians. Now it's Poland's turn to save her. This is how history works. The balance of power shifts over time, and we must be ready to make the right decisions. There's immense power in historical events, so we better be good now, to get to the good that comes later. It's necessary for her to leave tonight."

The ambassador keeps staring at me with sweets in his mouth. Then he nods 'yes'.

The psychologist hugs me and says, "I love you. Take care. Life has a lot in store for you. Get away from this mess."

She leaves in tears, and I remain alone with the employees of the Polish Embassy. Memories of the times the Polish psychologist helped me flash before my eyes. Even flashes of the dream in which she gave me a machine gun and asked me to kill anyone I had held grudges against, and I killed everyone including her. As I think back on all we've been through together, my glands explode, and the beard grows out.

The ambassador looks at me curiously. "Don't worry, we are going to help you find a new home."

As the ambassador approaches me, all the employees watch my beard grow. They are shocked. A woman who is a man, or a man wearing a veil. I feel heat in my throat. Time stops as he stares at me. We get closer to death from the day we are born, and every day along the way we must be willing to destroy something to move forward.

The ambassador says, "You can choose any country you want. Where would you like to live?"

I remember Natasha telling me all about the Old Port in Montreal, Canada. With all their eyes watching me, I feel like it is time to go. Danger has found me again, and now I have to leave the house where I grew up against my will. The home where I played with Setayesh, where I counted the centipede's feet and watched the boys ride bicycles. Where we took soda from Ali's store. Ali was so generous. He never told anyone about how we stole the soda.

Canada Dry, that was the name of our yellow-coloured soda! Now that I am about to leave forever, I see this memory as a sign from Setayesh. I want to go to the land of my favorite soda as a kid, and eat brunch along one of its streets. I want to make up for the unopened bottle of Canada Dry that Setayesh and I stole from Ali's store but didn't have a bottle opener so we could drink and cool off. I can still see it on the ground on the football field.

"Canada," I say. "Montreal."

"Okay then," the Polish ambassador says indifferently as he writes my future down on a form. "It won't be easy, as the Canadian Embassy in Iran is closed. But I have my own contacts. Don't worry."

I will never see my parents again. There is no way

back. Goodbye, my homeland. Goodbye, little centipedes, bicycles, and muddy balls on the football fields. Goodbye, beautiful mosques in the neighbourhood. Goodbye, beautiful streets in the north of Tehran. Goodbye, Jordan Street. Goodbye, villas that have been replaced with apartments.

Goodbye, Maman and Baba. Goodbye, Sara!

But which Sara?

PART FOUR

Difference

1

I'M IN MONTREAL. I HAD always assumed Canada was snowy with igloos everywhere. I assumed it would smell like the freshly opened suitcase at Natasha's house. We assume we're going to find Heaven, and there'll be no more suffering. We assume that all streets are clean and nobody litters, that there are no poor or homeless people. People in Montreal assume that my whole life is war and misery, even though millions of people live in Iran, and just like everywhere else, they have both good and bad days. Here there are no signs of igloos. Montreal has heat, and Iran is not limited to deserts. Nothing is absolute.

I live in a hotel room near a beautiful mountain. It is being paid for by the Polish Embassy, which has offered me to let me live here until they can provide me with a house. My room has green and yellow wallpaper. Every room in the hotel is named after a month. Mine is large, and it has floor-to-ceiling windows and an old bathtub that's deep enough to drown in. Every morning the hotel staff brings me breakfast. It is nothing like the breakfast my Maman gives us. You can get anything you want in this city.

I lie on my king-size bed in this clean suite and stare out at the Saint Lawrence River. My growing number of followers, especially now that I have left Iran and my life is no longer in danger, warms my heart. When this many people validate you, it means that you exist, and you are good. It means that just like a tiny branch of a tree that rises above others and reaches the clouds, I have risen above the streets of our dead-end neighbourhood and all its discrimination and conflicts, and now everyone can see me.

I spend all of my time on social media, counting the number of likes and comments. I have reached a million followers in just one week. From the TV to the newspapers here, I am all over the media and all the TV hosts want to interview me. They see me as a lab rat, a phenomenon to research. I occasionally counsel people, and I love being at the centre of attention. Westerners find my story surprising and often say, "You have a unique perspective!"

I talk to my fans about God, the God that I have known. This is my way of fighting years and years of discrimination. Somebody becomes the first female mayor, and somebody else becomes the first Black president or the first woman ever to go into space. We look at what they mean to the world, but we rarely ever ask if they are kind or nice. We give too much credit to what we see and hear.

I am teased for this by all the women who live inside me. But they are also really happy. It's like finally one of us has made it, found a way through all the men and through thousands of years of oppression. They sometimes grumble, but they can no longer control me, they can no longer scream and they can no longer silence me because what I hear from my audience, who also see themselves in me, is louder than they are.

It is summer here. Whenever I am all by myself, I lie down and stretch my legs against the cool tiles of the bathroom wall. I remove my veil and loosen my scarf. I touch my face and feel my skin, rough with large pores as a result of the beard growing in and out.

I live the life of a princess. People send me money from all over the world to be their prophetess. The Canadian government has grown interested in my story. The Polish Embassy has hired me a speech therapist to work on my stutter.

The first ever prophetess! My audience has given me this name. I would never claim such a title. My lawyer tells me that, here in the West, women are more valued. But even if they are, why would they also see themselves in me?

One day during an interview a journalist asks, "What gender do you identify with?"

"What kind of question is that?" I say to my translator.

The journalist says, "I mean do you see yourself as genderless or non-binary?"

All the women in me, who have come a long way, laugh at this. They say being a woman is absolute misery, and those who are born even a little bit male should hold on to that privilege. This is the outcome of thousands of years of what men have done to us. The man inside me has finally learned to speak for himself. He eats with us. He sings with us. He has his own privacy, his own needs. He needs to hide himself or sometimes express himself just like others inside me. Sometimes he needs to scream, shout, or speak. He grows my beard and pulls it back. This is what scares people. I am a woman who has been assaulted by men many times throughout history. My defence is to become a man during encounters with them.

But I am a woman. Not just one, but millions.

2

I CAN USE THE EXPENSIVE new smartphone they bought me to call Iran. Maman picks up the phone. I remain silent. To her, I still can't speak.

"Sara, darling, are you okay? I'm glad you called!" she cries.

Baba takes the phone. "Sara, we were so worried about you! The Polish woman told us that you were leaving. I saw your videos, darling. Why didn't you tell us that you were so important?"

Maman takes the phone back. "Bravo, my brave little girl. Bravo! You made the right choice by leaving. It is our fault that we haven't really seen you since Setayesh has been gone. Now take your sister's revenge upon them!"

"Upon who?" Baba asks.

Maman screams, "That's all your fault!"

I understand why Maman is so angry. I understand that she can't take it anymore, and just like each and every one of the women in me with their own individual story, Maman is one of them. Maybe she is in me, screaming, crying for revenge across centuries.

Maman says the ceiling of our house is leaking and that the mice have taken over. She says that she is scared to walk around the house without shoes on. I want to tell her that mice do not go away whether you have shoes on or not, but then I realize covering yourself gives you the kind of confidence that keeps danger away. I remember that during nights in Tehran when I couldn't sleep because of the hissing of cockroaches, I would pull a blanket over my head and feel like I was in the safest place in the world.

Maman says Baba has stopped taking opium, and they're lonely. She says everything has changed, and nothing will ever be the same again.

Even though they can't see it, I blow Maman and Baba a kiss, and I hang up the phone.

The people of this place worship me. They want to know my opinion on women's rights and animal rights and global warming and the death penalty. I come from a different world. I have no idea what to say. I go back and forth to meetings and blame the politicians for all the warfare and inequality in the world. I also say nice things, the beautiful things I hear daily from the people around me. They hear their own words from me and cheer for me and call me a brave young woman who fights for justice and equality, breaks taboos, and has become a role model for women. There are a lot of women who are encouraged by me. There are a lot of women who admire me for my resilience in the face of past troubles.

I wish I could always see what was on the other side of the curtain. The world changes, and changes my world with it. All these people and social networks try to change my destiny, while asking me to change theirs through my speeches and prayers. They want to hear me speak about the rapid warming of Northern Canada near the North Pole, whether I agree with policies, whether I like certain politicians or not, about my favourite colour and season, my morning routine. They write editorials about my speeches in newspapers and on social media.

Meanwhile, people in Iran have started taking selfies with my parents whenever they see them on the streets. They send me the photos. Even people here who see me on Sainte-Catherine Street ask for selfies. No matter where they are, people are the same. However, the only thing that matters to me is that, for these people, I have an identity. Without networks and reporters, I wouldn't exist for any of them.

3

BECAUSE A LOT OF PAGES on social media are talking about me, I've been invited to one of the prime minister's sessions with parliament. Members of parliament are going to share their country's problems with me to see what I have to offer as advice in return. I don't know English, and I haven't heard many of the terms they speak of, even after they're translated for me. I never finished school, and I am a young adult who never had a childhood. I jumped right into adulthood, and now my unwanted fame has me addressing political, economic, and social issues.

The women in me want something different every day. One day they want me to make statements against men, the next they ask me to disgrace anyone who has done me wrong, and after that they want to scream in front of the cameras and tell the world to fear their revenge.

Every morning I wake up for others, for the number of likes on social media and their comments, whether compliments or insults. The first thing I do every morning is think about what to say that day. What can I record today? Today I'll light a candle in front of the camera and cry for Setayesh. Today I'll tell them that one of the voices inside me is Setayesh, a kid who became the victim of an ignorant man's hunger for power. We must kill the hunger for power in people. I must insult the power-hungry as much as I can.

I turn on the camera. I light candles in every corner of the room. It satisfies me to post on social media and encourage people to insult whomever I decide needs insulting. I'll ask them to curse the power-hungry and destroy them with our unity. Everyone curses. Even the ones who swear at me have someone who swears at them.

I see people, one by one, coming online to watch my live video. Everyone's cursing in their language. All the languages in the world. Setayesh screams from deep within me, in the virtual presence of the whole world, just like she did on the day Uncle Moji was executed. She doesn't say anything. She only wants to be free, just like a genie trapped in a magic lamp whose only wish is to be free while obeying everybody else's wishes. Even without words, Setayesh's voice is all over the city. The people watching us online can't distinguish between my voice and Setayesh's, and yet they scream, "Hooray!"

The fact that people listen to me gives me power. I chant "Death to assailants!" and this virtual screaming makes me feel good. I am the good one, and the assailants are the bad ones. The people of the world have gathered to say "We're good and they're bad!" just like our neighbours did for Uncle Moji's execution.

It's getting late and I'm done with my daily social-media duties in the hotel near the Old Port. I've created, recorded, and posted new videos, making people laugh and cry as I talk about the other world. They love life. They love watching people like me. I need them to exist, and they need me to forget about themselves. I suck their youth and their energy out of them, and they chant, "Hooray!" They like and praise me. Peaceful coexistence.

Another day is over. If not for the videos I post or the visits I make for money, I would never leave the hotel at all.

4

My new translator is a Canadian who speaks my language. Somebody told me there are no actual Canadians in Canada, but I think otherwise. This country is the collection of all its residents. You can be Iranian and still be considered Canadian. You can be non-Canadian and Canadian at the same time, as simple as that. I think it's the beauty of this country.

The new translator is a middle-aged woman whose eyes look like those of the old woman inside me. The way she dresses is just like other women, but her behaviour is similar to the man in me. She is not Iranian. She doesn't need men in her life to have her freedoms. She shows no sign of trying to appeal to anyone. She is unlike anyone I've ever known.

"What's your name?" I ask.

"Iranian name or Canadian name?" she says.

"You have an Iranian name?"

She laughs and tells me her Québécois name is Charles, her English name is Charlie, and ever since she learned Persian, she has picked up the Persian name Shadi.

"But I only have one name."

"Virtual Prophetess!" she laughs.

"No, I only have one name, the name by which my family and Setayesh called me. A name that any woman in the world can have. Sara."

"Your name is Sara?"

"You mean you didn't know my name?"

"Nobody knows your name. To us, you are the Virtual Prophetess," Charlie says. "By the way, I'd be happy to translate your posts into English and French."

"How did you learn to speak Persian so well?"

She tells me she's been to Iran. She met an Iranian man many years ago and got married, and that's why she learned Persian. She can cook Persian food and recite Hafiz's and Rumi's poems. She loves the ancient capital of Persepolis, the streets of Isfahan, the old neighbourhoods in Tehran, and Yazd, the oldest mud-brick city in the world.

She asks me why I've chosen Canada. I know exactly the answer she wants to hear. But my response is more practical than that. "I just chose the first place that would have me. I didn't leave by choice. Maybe my conditions were better than those of others, but it was still a matter of life and death. Also, I have loved Canada Dry ever since I was a child."

"But what about Québec?" she asks with her sweet Québécois accent. "Why did you come here?"

"My mother cleans rich people's houses for a living. We once went to a house in uptown Tehran, where Maman was the help for a party. The family had a girl my age. I went to her room and we played pretend. We pretended we were two Mamans in Montreal, in the Old Port. I knew nothing about the world outside our poor neighbourhood. I thought that Heaven was a place just like their house, their neighbourhood and their cars. I watched men and women drinking at that party, together, wearing whatever they wished, and I realized that there was a world outside of the one I knew."

Charlie looks at me and laughs. She touches my veil and says, "It's good that the hijab is not mandatory here, but you've chosen it yourself."

"Nobody has seen my hair since I was seven years old," I say, "not even Maman."

"But in Iran, nobody wears the hijab at home!" Charlie says, surprised.

I offer no further explanation. I grab my veil so that my hair won't pop out. I gaze at the church across the street from my hotel. We are both silent. The women in me are silent too, though they sometimes whisper to one another. None of them know what they want. Neither do I.

5

WHAT IS IT LIKE BEING a social media prophetess?

I live for others. I live in the presence of others. I live-stream and talk to my fans, whose numbers increase day by day. Reporters call me from all around the world. I make videos, give speeches and lectures. I am an animal lover, an altruist, and a kind being. I pray. I talk about men's and women's rights, politics, the environment, and the beauty of life.

I have a thousand women and one man in me, each of whom speaks a different language. I have Charlie beside me. My Persian fans adore her cute accent, and the whole world sees her at the side of an Instagram celebrity.

People will always need to make a god out of some-one, to follow, to adopt as a lifestyle. I also need them.

It's a win-win situation. But their existence is becoming insufficient. How many likes can I collect? How many views? How much encouragement? How many insults? I need more. Waking up and getting in front of a camera to talk about my usual subjects has become repetitive. My body and my soul want other things.

Charlie suggests we get tattoos. It could be interesting. It could get us a lot more viewers. "We can get a tattoo of one of Rumi's or Khayyam's poems here." Charlie points to her legs, as she already has a few tattoos on her arms.

I look at her, and she comes to her senses.

"You can't show your body, but maybe you can get a tattoo on your face."

"Why do you like tattoos so much?" I ask.

While she answers my question, I write a post on social media: "If you were to get a tattoo of a poem, which poem would you choose?" I get hundreds of comments a minute, and my phone keeps ringing with notifications. I put my phone in my pocket and listen to Charlie. She says that she grew up in a strict Catholic family, and had to be home before six p.m., be neat and tidy, and always pray before meals. When she turned eighteen, she left home, and to prove to herself that she could make her own decisions, she got tattoos all over her arms. Now she's married to a Jewish-Iranian man and has visited all the beautiful churches and mosques in Iran. By disagreeing with her family she affirms her existence. She owns her body and can do whatever she wants with it.

We keep on talking as we go out to find a tattoo parlour. I tell her that, in Iran, women's bodies belong to their husbands, fathers, brothers and the government. She laughs and says the whole world needs awareness. At the tattoo parlour, there's a man with purple hair and multiple piercings standing behind the counter. He recognizes me. He gets closer, but I say, "No. Charlie, ask for a woman."

Charlie grabs my hand and takes me into a room where we each lie on a tattoo bed. A young woman with multi-coloured hair approaches us. Her whole face is tattooed. "Having you here is an honour," she says.

Charlie asks her about the most popular tattoos. She replies, "Yin and Yang."

"Yin and Yang?" I ask. One of the women in me screams that she knows about that.

"It's the symbol of the dark and light, women and men, and everything contradictory in this world," the tattoo artist says.

I look at her.

She tries to simplify her explanation. "For example, there's a man in every woman and a woman in every man."

I look at the tattoos all over her body. "Why do you have so many tattoos?" I ask.

She looks a bit ashamed. I suddenly remember high

school, when I ruthlessly assaulted my classmates and looked for tweezers and their boyfriends' photos in their backpacks. I still see them, insulting me in social media comments and talking about their unpleasant experiences with me. They're probably just jealous now that I have become somebody superior to them. I still remember the shame in their eyes, as if they had committed a great sin.

"You know, after the first time you get a tattoo, you'll start to like the pain on your skin caused by the needles, and you'll want to experience it again," the tattoo artist says. "It's a constant but not at all severe pain that I've become addicted to."

I look to Charlie. "Don't be scared, it's not that painful," she says.

I ask Charlie to take a selfie of us. She suggests, since we don't have much time, that we pick the first poem we read in the comments fans have left on my post. I click on my page, and the first comment is from an Iranian fan named Raayan.

Come, come, whoever you are, come again.
If a pagan, a magus, an idolater, come again.
Our threshold is not for despairing:
If a thousand times you break faith, come again.
                                    –Abu Saeid Abukheir

"Okay," I say. "We're going to tattoo that one."

We take selfies: me, Charlie, and the tattoo artist. The tattoo artist says I can get a small tattoo next to my eye or a bigger tattoo that covers my whole face. Charlie says a tattoo next to my eye will be more painful, but also very unique. So I ask for a small tattoo on my forehead, above my right eye, written in Persian. Charlie reads more of the comments while I lie down to get started.

"Please share more photos of yourself!"

"Your words calm me down."

"You are beautiful!"

"I love finger tattoos. Get a finger tattoo!"

"Excuse me, but now that you've experienced being in the male form, which one is better? Male or female?"

"Now that you're rich, will you lend me some money?"

"Please make statements on LGBTQ rights, and send messages to politicians. We are human beings, just like you."

"Do you wear more comfortable clothes at home?"

"Why are you so good?"

"I can see the poem you've chosen for your tattoo. Do you know its meaning? To God, we all exist regardless of religion or beliefs, and no group is superior to others. I hope you know what you're inking on your body."

Charlie and I look at each other. I'm scared. There's a scary side to being who we are. If we're all the same, why do I get so many fans? Why should they like me? Why do organizations and the media spend so much time promoting me? I am getting a statement against myself inked on my forehead, claiming I am not different than others. I know it's true, but such a claim means losing everything. It means I don't exist anymore.

My weakness and the pain caused by the needles intensify. I faint, and suddenly all is black.

6

CHARLIE IS STANDING over my head. I open my eyes and see her looking down on me in what seems to be a different room than the one where we were get-ting the tattoos. This room smells like disinfectant.

"How do you feel?" Charlie asks"I'm fii…fiii…ne. What happened?"

"You lost consciousness."

"Give me my…my... ph…phone."

"You need to rest. The doctor said you probably fainted because of the pain from the needle and from fear."

"Oh…fear… This has happened to me on…once before, a fe…few years ago."

"Seriously?" the doctor says.

"It happened once, at school."

"Did you start speaking in Vietnamese that time too?"

"It…It's not Vietnamese, it's Polish."

"No. You kept repeating the same thing in Vietnamese, Lingala, and Swahili. You kept saying that you had to defend yourself when your country was attacked. You said the same thing several times in these languages."

"What are these languages?"

"Well, Vietnamese is obviously the language of Vietnam, Lingala is from Congo, and Swahili is spoken in Tanzania. Do you know where these countries are?"

"No, I've always been pretty bad at geography."

"You held your head very tightly."

"It happened last time too. Look, do you really speak all these languages?"

"No."

"Then how did you recognize them?"

The doctor hands me my phone. Videos of me lying on the ground, speaking these words in different languages have already gone viral. The people in me, and the countries in me, they're all frustrated because of the oppression they have dealt with. They scream for their rights at any given chance. Maybe one day they'll take their power back. I really hope they don't hold on to their anger until that day. I hope they don't choose revenge for justice. I hope they don't respond in the way they were treated. I feel dizzy. The whole world is watching a moment of my life in which I was not even present.

"Who recorded these videos?"

"I don't know," says Charlie, "maybe one of the tattoo artists who was here."

"And yo…you let th..them do it?"

"Have they done anything bad?"

"This is a personal and private moment in my life."

"I don't think you have a private life anymore. Things are getting out of control. I can't stop people from filming you in public."

I look out the window.

"But this is good," says Charlie. "It's an indicator of power. You belong to the whole world now."

I don't want to belong to the whole world. I want to choose what they see and what they don't see.

"Sara, didn't you work on your stutter?" Charlie asks. "It had gone away."

Have I unknowingly started stuttering again? I want to be alone. I want to disappear and go back to my hotel room, and be all alone.

"Of course you were speaking perfectly when you were unconscious, but I don't know why you're anxious now!" Charlie continues, as if she's speaking to herself.

I feel a flash of heat. I get up and open the hospital room door. A lot of people are waiting for me outside, but I run so fast that none of them even have time to take their phones out of their pockets for a video. Once we're in the back of the car, the driver speeds off.

Back at the hotel, in the bathroom, I take off all my clothes. That's when I notice the lines on my forehead. The tattoo artist didn't get to finish the tattoo, and all it says in Persian is, "Come, come again."

7

Among the people who gather outside my hotel, I spot a man. Unlike other people who are there praying and lighting candles for me, he just stares at my window with an innocent look in his eyes. He catches my attention after I recover from the fainting episode that went viral. From that day on, everywhere I go, I see him among my fans, often in the front row.

People like him are everywhere—devoted fans who are infatuated with famous people and think they can have part of us for themselves. But he has to know that no man can ever have me. That any man who comes close triggers my body. My success is based on my loneliness. No man can play a part in what I do.

One day I am scheduled to do a live interview and put out a new statement for my fans. I am used to speaking at recitals, and thanks to my speech therapist I have recovered from my fainting episode and can now speak without a stutter once again, at least in Persian. Charlie is happy to take care of the rest. Everyone knows her as my closest confidant.

Reporters are there taking photos of me. The host of the interview introduces me as the first prophetess in history, whose life was once in danger in her home country and has now been saved by the Western world. They recognize me as a virtual prophetess and influencer, but deep down I feel that I am not a messenger, and I have done nothing more than seek protection and peace. Still, it is so satisfying to see how freely I speak about these subjects on television—how freely I can speak about my followers, and how a woman has finally become a leader in this world. They want me to talk about the dangers that threaten me. Meanwhile, all the women in me remember their homes being invaded, their uncertainties, their assaults and their wars. The truth is a game, and I am its winner. But the truth won't change anything: I'm not a messenger from God, and I wouldn't be here and have this many followers if I weren't a woman.

Now that I've noticed him, I always see this man in the crowd. I feel like he can see my truth, even though no one else can. He smiles at me as if no one else is around. Who is he? He holds up a sign in Persian. It's a poem by Hafiz:

For years my heart inquired of me
Where Jamshid's sacred cup might be,
And what was in its own possession
It asked from strangers, constantly.

Everyone sees me read the sign. The interviewer looks at me as she pulls her long blonde hair aside. All eyes turn to me. I freeze. How can he read my mind? And know the doubt I feel? As I stand there on that open stage listening to the interviewer talk on and on, I think once again how I no longer want to be an object of propaganda. I don't even want to be someone who other people rely on. I have spent a lifetime being traumatized by idolization. I lost my sister, my home, my country, and now these people here are idolizing me still. How should I respond to these people who have made whatever they want out of me?

The man stands up and leaves. I do not speak. Charlie, as my translator and coach, stares at me with concern, as if to communicate, "Say something!"

"It's not time to speak," I say, needing to finish the sentence I started a while ago. "It's time to act."

What the hell did I just say? Where did that come from?

I leave the stage. No one in the audience moves. No one talks.

8

THERE IS PERSISTENT KNOCKING at my door, but I won't open it. I am a disgrace to all my followers and all the propaganda they want. The guilt has found its way back to me again. Nothing is the way it should be. Everything has gone wrong. No one should ever control people or silence them. I, who have lived one hundred and fourteen years and observed war after war, am now an entertainer for people who are drawn to trivial things. All superstars who become famous have a job, each in their own unique way, to distract people so that their rulers can dictate in peace.

I look at the crowd outside my hotel window. The man is there gazing back at me as if he knows I am looking for him. Who am I to him? I step away from the window and lie down on the bed. I must have fallen asleep, because when I open my eyes it's already dark. I open Instagram. They're talking about my mesmerizing speech. The host of the show has declared my speech the most influential one of its kind in the past twenty years. There's an image of Charlie under the headline which reads: "The initial reactions to the Prophetess's commandments."

How shallow! The headline has turned me into someone who is savvy in the ways of the West. Everyone praises me without even questioning what I say. People prefer security over freedom, which is why we'll do anything to be safe, even if it means being captivated. The easiest way to security is to close our eyes and make legends accountable for everything.

Outside, there's a crowd still gathered in the dark, holding candles, shedding tears. I feel guilty.

I don't want to lie. I owe these victimized people a truth. I have always been repressed and ignored. I have always stood in the shadows. And now that I have the chance to be seen, nothing feels honest anymore.

When I look out the window again, I see the man once more. He's sitting on a hill tending a fire pit, beyond the lawn where my followers have gathered. This time he has a new sign. He's asking me to come over and sit next to the fire with him. I already feel its heat. I want to meet him, but I know that as soon as I get close, my beard will start to grow. He's not ashamed of anything. Men can be so interesting, honest, and precise. There can be good things about men, these strange creatures! I am so curious to get to know him. I am so curious to know why he seems so attractive, so mysterious, and yet so unattainable to me.

I know that if I tell my team about it, they won't let me go out. They will tell me it's dangerous for me to be alone with my fans. But he isn't dangerous. He isn't a fan either. He has a message for me, I can feel it; maybe that's why I want to meet him. I see him laugh in the distance and hint that it's getting late for me to come have tea with him. He points to his watch and his kettle, and mimics drinking tea. I like his laugh, even though I can't hear it. He looks pretty confident. I want to go but I am afraid.

I touch my throat, which is hot and ready to explode. I put on a hat and cover my face with a scarf. I exit through the hotel's loading dock, so my fans won't see me, and enter the crowd anonymously. It's my first time going out in a sweatsuit and a hat. In these clothes, I am not the Sara I was before. Or maybe the previous versions aren't Sara, and this is who I really am.

As I get closer to the hill, I feel the fire's heat even more. I can see the man from afar, waiting for me. My glands are about to burst, like they already know I'm about to have tea with a man and communicate with him in a way I never have with men before. As I imagine us laughing or taking a walk, hair glands bubble under my skin. I close my eyes for a second and hear a happy upbeat song. I can't figure out if it's real and coming from the gathering below, or a dream. I want to dance a Persian dance. But I don't know how. I feel the breeze on my face, and my hands go cold, so I put them against my throat to cool it off.

I keep on walking. Soon there is nothing higher above us than darkness. I can smell him. I must be pretty close. There's a smile on my face and joy in my heart despite the coolness of the breeze. To my surprise, my face is no longer hot. My glands no longer feel like exploding. I am free. I have come to meet a man who has invited me for tea. I open my eyes, and there he is—right in front of me—smiling.

"Hi, Sara! I'm Raayan."

9

IT FEELS LIKE HEAVEN UP HERE. It feels like the moment when all the secrets of the world are revealed, like the day you die and get all your answers all at once. You can see everything from here, every person, every house. People are close, eating dinner, walking, brushing their teeth, and falling asleep in front of the TV. This is where you can count the exact number of a centipede's feet. The world is so big from here. Everything is so close.

Raayan hands me a cup of tea. "It's pretty cold tonight," he says.

"Yeah."

"I see you couldn't get your tattoo completed. That poem I sent to you was great."

"You sent it to me?" The first comment on my post… I remember. "What is going on here?"

"I also have Canada Dry," says Raayan. "You want one? Or is tea good? Don't look at me like that! I know you love Canada Dry!"

"How did you…"

"Make yourself comfortable."

"… know?"

"You don't remember? How you used to steal them as a kid? You weren't surrounded by so many people back then. You were all by yourself! And sometimes with Setayesh! Your hair was long and you pulled it back…"

"When I was a kid?"

"Yeah! You don't remember taking Canada Dry from the store?"

This man knows everything about my past. "Who are you? A prophet?"

He laughs. "A prophetess looking for a prophet. How ironic."

"Who are you? Tell me."

"It's human. They make you famous, and you want to make me famous. What we don't have we want to project onto others to escape the responsibility. I am Raayan. You took Canada Dry from my father's store. It is not complicated."

Those were the days that Setayesh and I were always together. Those were the days when Setayesh was alive and so was Uncle Moji. And Ali too.

"Ali was your father? Why did I never ask your name?"

"When you don't care about someone, you forget their name."

"So you remembering my name means you cared about me?"

"At some point everyone cared about you. The whole neighbourhood will remember your names forever—you, Setayesh, and Uncle Moji. I never got to see you and tell you how sorry I was…"

"Why do we still call him Uncle Moji?"

"I guess he was Uncle Moji to us kids, but a murderer and a rapist to the law."

"I suppose you knew Loqman too. I got to see him before I moved away."

"Oh, I guess you're pretty mad at him."

"Mad at him? I don't know… How did you find me?"

"I didn't find you. I just saw you all over social media, and your hotel was near my residence."

"So you are a refugee?"

"Yes."

"We never paid your dad for those Canada Dry sodas."

"And that's what you remember of Canada. The sodas!"

"I remember you were the only person who told me I had a good voice, Raayan! The only person!"

We both laugh and then stare at the city in silence for a while.

Finally, he says, "You should probably leave. They will get worried. I should leave too. I hope to see you again."

I don't want him to leave yet. This man is the dark spot in me that I have never seen before. He is calm. He is sure of himself and knows what he wants. He is not afraid to seek refuge in something else. "Why did you come looking for me?" I say. "Why did you write that sign?"

"Because I know where you come from. I know the difference between the two Saras. Anyway, what's done is done…"

"So what did you do that made you end up a refugee?"

"Sometimes even breathing is a political activity."

"You want to take a walk?" I say. I want to take a walk with him. I want to take a walk and find myself, and find my femininity alongside his masculinity, the kind of femininity Setayesh had when she pulled her hair back. I loved that about her.

"I like that you're yourself around me," Raayan says. "Sometimes you just need to be completely yourself."

"What do you mean? How do you know what or who I am? I have thousands of selves."

"Look! Nothing is growing to cover your face and protect you."

He is right. My hair glands are not acting up.

We walk along the top of the hill overlooking the city. It is cool in the dark and people down in the streets are visible to us as ants. They walk on the lines between mosaics, step on autumn leaves and smash centipedes that have one hundred and eighty-one pairs of feet, but are never punished for their crimes. From up here, everything looks different. Raayan takes my hand in his. And I say to myself that I wish I had let go sooner, let someone hold my hand, felt good. Who forbade all this beauty? I take a look at all the years I have deprived myself, and others, of all the great things in this world.

Raayan doesn't say anything, and I don't either. It's as if all the words have been spoken before, and the earth has heard it all a million times. We're walking in the dark, following paths between the trees and bushes. Now is a time to be present. Raayan moves forward, focused and determined, and I do the same, calm and a bit clumsy. It's a strange silence. I look back down the hill. There are people standing down there, staring back at me. I know them all. They are me and I am them. All the Setayeshes, the old women, the Nedas, Nasrins, Natashas, and Saras! They exist. They never disappear from this world. They're waving at us as we move forward. All the people who were present for Uncle Moji's execution are also there now. All those I had killed off in my dream are also down there, and it's as if I know none of them will chase me any longer. They don't live in me anymore. They no longer struggle. They don't want more blood for blood. More death for death. They just get smaller as Raayan and I move forward. Raayan doesn't know they're standing behind us. He sees my worried face searching for something behind me.

"Yeah, I know it is dark out here, but don't be scared," he says. "There's nothing behind us!" Then he adds, "I have to tell you something. I was responsible for executions during my mandatory military service."

I assume he's kidding. But his face goes sad, and he continues.

"I am a bad man."

"But you were forced," I reason.

"No."

"What do you mean, no?"

"In the beginning, I chose it. I thought I could take revenge on Uncle Moji and all the bad men, but after a while I understood each human being had his own story. The system wants to decide for us who dies, but there must always be a real person to carry out the act. That person was me. Now it is forever part of who I am."

There is a long silence. I know the feeling of participating in the handing out of larger judgments. Raayan says, "Before I go, we need to ride a bike. I want you to experience it."

"Before you go where?"

"I have to go. You will see."

"You mean you are going to leave?"

"Hey… I have something for you. I know a chalet outside the city. We can rent it for a while, and one day we can try magic mushrooms. Just a small amount."

"What is that?"

"Just a mushroom, but it's magic. I am not a fan of what I've done in my life, but you are not a fan of your life either, with all its do's and don'ts. Maybe once in your life you need to just let go and see what happens. Just once."

"Tell me why you want to leave."

"All illusions disappear one day."

10

WE TAKE THE MAGIC mushrooms. Soon we are bathed in delightful sunlight on a beautiful hill covered with green grass. No signs of snow. Not a cloud in the sky. We run through a meadow, and Raayan holds my hand as we run. My hair comes loose, fluttering in the wind. Along a riverbank we come across two bicycles, and beyond them there are two kids swimming in the river. Raayan says, "Let's take the bicycles and go for a ride. Hurry up! Before the kids get here!"

It was cold yesterday. Today's sunny. Am I awake? He throws me on a bicycle and leads the way. We laugh so hard and everything moves so fast that I forget to say I don't know how to ride a bicycle.

"Come on, hurry up! Pedal!"

He's moving away, and I have been laughing so hard that I keep pedaling without thinking about anything else! He has gotten farther away, and he keeps shouting, "Pedal! Faster! Faster! Faster!" I hear Setayesh's voice shout, "Higher!" I hear Loqman breathing. But nothing happens inside of me. I pedal, as the wind blows and takes with it the heavy weight of all these years. Gravity becomes nonexistent. I become weightless.

My hair gets in my face, and I pull it back just like Setayesh did. My hair is all white!

Raayan says, "Don't you feel free?"

He doesn't understand. No one understands a little girl who is abandoned, whose sister has left her, whose parents are busy with their own problems, whose classmates taunt her because she can't speak, whose teachers sigh because it's hard working with her. A girl who has no one in this world but her God and her beliefs. A girl who can't talk to anyone but her God. No one understands how religion makes a life full and provides her what she has never had. How religion is something we inherit. How it determines so much for us to make us a good child of God. And we struggle to remain the good children of God, even if we can't change the past. But we can let go of it and leave its weight in the wind.

"The past can be changed. Everyone who says it can't is wrong," I hear a voice inside me say. But it's not the old woman, not Setayesh, no one from my past. It's simply the voice of Sara, which I have not heard in so very long. "The past is both a pain and healing."

Sara is the first name of all women.

I see Loqman and Setayesh laughing on the swing, looking at us.

I hear Uncle Moji say, "You bastards! What are you doing? You filthy sinners!"

Fear appears in Loqman's and Setayesh's eyes.

Raayan and I laugh. We hear the kids coming our way.

"You thieves!"

"Pedal! Pedal! Faster! Faster!" he yells.

I pedal, and we breathe rapidly, still laughing. We can barely speak because of all the laughter. As we pedal away, I shout, without stuttering, "We promise to give your bicycles back!"

"Say it in English, you dummy!" Raayan shouts, laughing so hard.

We laugh again. I have forgotten to tell him that I don't speak English. And now the whole world is just an image, with no sound. Everything is silent, only my laugh echoes in my world. The beautiful sun passes through my eyes, the wind touches my face, and I keep pedalling gently, as if I'm flying away.

11

THE AIR IS HEAVY. Raayan is watching me from the crowd. His eyes keep saying, "Go on!"

I will always feel uncomfortable around people. I will never get used to their presence. For me, everything has taken place in an inner world. Since our bicycles landed on the ground, I find it difficult to make public speeches and answer repetitive questions. I am now a different Sara. I'm relearning who I am and where I come from, but the presence of all the women and the one man who live inside me gets in my way.

The journalist says, "So, yesterday someone hacked your pages, and your social media profiles are all offline. Before that happened, they wrote that you were not a prophetess and that you wanted to be yourself. Please, as the Virtual Prophetess, tell your fans that your pages were hacked and that you are still with them."

I look for Raayan as I stand up. I see him disappearing like a prophet, heading for the door. He goes away, just like he already told me he would. I want to ask him to stay, but I don't. I know he told me what I needed to hear. I experienced whatever I had to experience, and now it is my turn to act. Just like a prophet, he gave me a message and then left. If he did stay, he would say that people are not your friends or your enemies, but they are your masters. They are your prophets. This is how you know a prophet: his advice becomes your own.

I follow him with my eyes. He opens the door and leaves. Maybe we will meet again soon.

"My pages have not been hacked," I say.

People whisper.

"What do you mean, Prophetess?"

"I am not the Prophetess. I am not your Prophetess. I am not satisfying your curiosity. I am tired. There are lots of things you can discover. Life is short. My childhood is gone. Everything has a value because we believe it does. Let's believe in something and someone who deserves our trust."

People start to scream, clapping and whistling. Obviously, they think it's a part of my speech as the Virtual Prophetess. But I am tired. I want to reconnect with myself, have dinner with myself, know myself. I want to meet myself for the first time. I want to see what I want, what I really need. I who left my childhood in the past, who never lived it. I want to have my own voice. Restart. What does Sara want?

"Yes, I am the Prophetess, but I am not your Prophetess!" I say it loudly into the microphone, and I exit the conference.

Everything freezes. No one says anything. They will forget me soon enough, and they will find someone else to follow. Perhaps they think I'll disappear. They like things mysterious. But I am here and I see them. I see the revolutionaries who assassinated dictators without trials. I see the kids killed in wars, the refugees dead on beaches. I see the priests who raped little boys and talked about forgiveness of Christ every single Sunday. I see the kings who killed their own people and the governments who repressed their citizens. I see the fast-food chains that sell an early death and the people who buy it. I see the roosters who are forced to fertilize hens, by people who want to earn money from eggs. I see the First Nations and the Palestinians and everyone else who is homeless in their own home. I see parents who manipulate children and children who manipulate pets. I see. Nothing disappears.

"Hey, Sara, forget all that," Setayesh laughs. "Let's go play soccer in Uncle Moji's backyard."

I hear her voice everywhere.

I see my soul separating from my body. I see the Polish woman again, but she doesn't give me a gun this time. She just looks at me and asks me to stay with all my fans. I see Raayan, I see Maman, I see Baba. I see myself saying, "Let's not get lost in the trap of our eyes. No one looks that different from up here."

My soul flies above Montreal and away from this world. I see my soul bare: no tattoos, no shoes, no hijab, no clothes, no face and no white hair. From up here, everything is clearer, everything is the same colour, and everything has the same name. It all fits on the head of a pin. It all fits in an atom.

Everything is me. I am the centipede. The soul is the body. From up here, all voices are one. My voice and Setayesh's voice laughing.

ACKNOWLEDGEMENTS

If not for my mother teaching me to be strong and telling me stories about Oprah Winfrey, I would have never written this book. Without the unconditional support of Chadi Alhelou, Jacob Wren, Marina Ledig-Coelho, and Dimitri Nasrallah, *Prophetess* could not have been published, as English is not my mother tongue. Special thanks to a friend, without whom this book could not have been written in English in the first place. They asked me, with absolute humility, to not mention their name. Perhaps if they lived in a different country, I wouldn't have listened and mentioned their name anyway.

"Setayesh" was the name of an Afghan girl who was raped and murdered in Iran. In honour of all the innocent victims, I named my character after her, and I bow to all the women who fight in Iran and Afghanistan.

ESPLANADE
Books

Hungary-Hollywood Express : A novel by Éric Plamondon
[Translated from the French by Dimitri Nasrallah]
English is Not a Magic Language : A novel by Jacques Poulin
[Translated from the French by Sheila Fischman]
Tumbleweed : Stories by Josip Novakovich
A Three-Tiered Pastel Dream : Stories by Lesley Trites
Sun of a Distant Land : A novel by David Bouchet
[Translated from the French by Claire Holden Rothman]
The Original Face : A novel by Guillaume Morissette
The Bleeds : A novel by Dimitri Nasrallah
Nirliit : A novel by Juliana Léveillé-Trudel
[Translated from the French by Anita Anand]
The Deserters : A novel by Pamela Mulloy
Mayonnaise : A novel by Éric Plamondon
[Translated from the French by Dimitri Nasrallah]
The Teardown : A novel by David Homel
Apple S : A novel by Éric Plamondon
[Translated from the French by Dimitri Nasrallah]
Aphelia : A novel by Mikella Nicol
[Translated from the French by Lesley Trites]
Dominoes at the Crossroads : Stories by Kaie Kellough
Swallowed : A novel by Réjean Ducharme
[Translated from the French by Madeleine Stratford]
Book of Wings : A novel by Tawhida Tanya Evanson
The Geography of Pluto : A novel by Christopher DiRaddo
The Family Way : A novel by Christopher DiRaddo
Fear the Mirror : Stories by Cora Siré
Open Your Heart : A novel by Alexie Morin
[Translated from the French by Aimee Wall]
Hotline : A novel by Dimitri Nasrallah
Prophetess : A novel by Baharan Baniahmadi